# The Fortkeeper's Keys

**Angeli Perrow**

*Don't forget your flashlight!*

*Angeli Perrow*

**Mustang Books**

**Cover format by Michele Bonin**

## DEDICATION

For my brother Michael with love

# ACKNOWLEDGEMENTS

My thanks to Michael Curtis of the wonderful
Union River Book & Toy Co. in Ellsworth, Maine
for suggesting a Key Mystery be set at Fort Knox

**www.unionrivertoys.com**

My thanks to Roger Bennatti and Leon Seymour
of Friends of Fort Knox for checking my 'fort facts'
and answering my many questions

# READ THIS PREVIEW. . . IF YOU DARE!

To Nick, the fort seemed like a giant maze with its long dark passages and mysterious rooms. He and his cousin headed up another set of steps with a sign announcing Enlisted Men's Quarters over the doorway.

Inside they found a big wooden box on legs beside a wide wooden shelf with a sign that said Kneading Table. Behind it a brick wall contained open iron doors of different sizes, some just big enough for a person to crawl into.

"This is the bakery," Mandy said.

"Reminds me of Hansel and Gretel," Nick commented. "The witch in the gingerbread house would have loved this oven. She could have baked a dozen kids at the same time!"

"Right, Nick," Mandy said, rolling her eyes. "Aunt Julie said it was never used. When troops were here during the Spanish-American War, they set up field kitchens outside for cooking. It took 400 loaves of bread a day to feed them all."

"Heh, heh, that's a lot of dough,' said Nick. "The ovens are cool though. Just peek in and make sure Sergeant Hegyi isn't baking muffins."

Mandy snorted and shined her light into one of the dark holes. "Well, silly, he wouldn't be *in* the oven."

"With ghosts you never know. They can be anywhere." To the right of the ovens, he found a narrow passageway that slotted in between two brick walls with a low granite lintel overhead. His flashlight illuminated it for a few yards and then the tunnel twisted out of sight. Beyond the entrance, the walls became stone, as if they had been chiseled out of the bedrock. The floor was hard-packed earth. It reminded Nick of the tunnels in the ghost mine in Nevada near where he lived—the *haunted* mine. "Where do you think this goes?" he asked. He wasn't about to find out. Who knew what might be around that corner?

His cousin joined him and peered in. "Let's follow it."

"Uh, you go ahead. Ladies first," Nick said. "Plus you're smaller than me. I don't want to get stuck."

"Yeah, right," she said, starting into the passageway.

In a moment, she disappeared around the bend, but Nick could still see the glow of her light. "What do you see?" he called.

No answer.

"Mandy?"

Her light vanished.

"Mandy, answer me!"

Shoot, he *really* didn't want to go in there. Did she fall into a trap? Trip and knock herself out? Get kidnapped by the ghost? He supposed he had to rescue her. Nick took a deep breath, gathering his courage. He took a few steps into the tunnel. . . and then a few more. He had reached the bend and couldn't see beyond it. "Mandy?" he said again.

"Ooooo," wailed an unearthly voice.

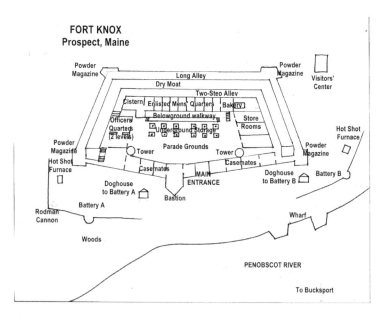

**FORT KNOX**
Prospect, Maine

Powder Magazine

Powder Magazine

Visitors' Center

Long Alley

Dry Moat

Two-Step Alley

Cistern

Enlisted Mens' Quarters

Bakery

Belowground walkway

Officers Quarters (2 levels)

Underground Storage

Store Rooms

Hot Shot Furnace

Powder Magazine

Parade Grounds

Powder Magazine

Hot Shot Furnace

Tower

Tower

Casemates

Casemates

MAIN ENTRANCE

Doghouse to Battery B

Battery B

Doghouse to Battery A

Bastion

Rodman Cannon

Battery A

Wharf

Woods

PENOBSCOT RIVER

To Bucksport

8

## Chapter 1.  Footsteps in the Fort

"No more coffins, Nick," his cousin Mandy said. She blew a stray wisp of light brown hair out of her eyes and crossed her arms.

"Why not?" he said, lifting the lid of another box. "I want to see what's inside." He shined his flashlight on the body. "Cool."

"Not really," she replied. "If you've seen one dummy, you've seen them all."

He narrowed his eyes at her.  "Is that an insult? What's the matter with you anyway? I thought you liked creepy things."

Mandy kicked at the base of a gravestone. "This is different. It doesn't feel right to have all this fake stuff here. It kind of spoils the *real* atmosphere of the fort."

Nick raised an eyebrow. "Oh, yeah? I think it's awesome. I couldn't believe it when your Aunt Julie said we could look around the fort by ourselves. It's cool that she's a volunteer here. We get our own private preview of Fright at the Fort."

"This is pretty tame," she said. "Just props. On the actual night, there are spooky sounds and actors who jump out at you in gruesome costumes."

"Sweet," he said. "I can't wait."

Mandy rolled her eyes. "It's okay, I guess, that they have it at Halloween time, but in July too? It's such a big money maker in the fall, the Friends of the Fort decided to add this summer event. That's one too many."

"Don't be a wet blanket," Nick said to his cousin. "It's just for fun."

"Aren't you interested in the *real* history of Fort Knox?" she asked in an exasperated voice.

"Sure," he replied, flicking his finger at a big, hairy spider that dangled above the coffin. "Tell me about the battles."

"Um, well. . . there weren't any."

"Huh? A fort with no battles—that's lame." She scowled at him. "Aunt Julie said that in the War of 1812, the British took over or

10

destroyed a lot of the settlements along the Penobscot River. Even after we won the war, they were threatening to invade because they didn't agree with the boundary between Canada and the U.S. So people kept asking the government to build a fort for protection. By the time they got around to it, the threat was over. But Fort Knox was used to train Civil War soldiers and was manned during the Spanish-American War for a little while. So it was important. Oh, and there were *lots* of cannons."

"Cannons?" Nick repeated with sudden interest. "Now we're talking. Are there any left?"

"There are a few. Come on, I'll show you one." Mandy led the way through a series of vaulted rooms called casemates connected by granite steps going up to each level. One side of each casemate opened onto the fort's inner courtyard called the parade grounds and the other side was part of the thick outer wall.

Nick looked around as he followed his cousin. Each casemate had an arched ceiling of bricks, blotched here and there with hardened white drips like the inside of a cave. Two deep window openings faced with stone offered a view of the wide Penobscot River below and the town of Bucksport, Maine on the opposite shore. Nick stuck his arm through one of them to see how thick the wall was. His fingertips could just reach the outside. *Must be at least three feet thick*, he thought. Even without battles, he decided it was a cool place. But he liked teasing Mandy—she could be so serious at times.

"Here you go," Mandy said, as she entered the next section, "one of your favorite things."

A large black cannon on a metal carriage dominated the space, its muzzle aimed at a wall opening. Nearby, a pyramid of cannon balls lay ready for action.

Nick sighted down the cannon through the porthole. He pretended to light a fuse. "Ba-boom!" he yelled. "I just knocked a seagull off Colonel Buck's gravestone over there in Bucksport!"

He saw a smile form on Mandy's face before she could stop it. "You're crazy, Nick," she said. "Let's go."

They walked through a few more arches to one corner of the fort's grassy parade grounds. In a stone tower, a spiral staircase wound upward.

"What's up there?" Nick asked, peering in. It seemed kind of mysterious, like something from a medieval castle.

"That goes to the top of the fort. You can see in every direction up there. It must have been a great lookout spot for the soldiers."

"Let's go!" said Nick, eager to check it out.

"Later," Mandy replied. "First, there's something I want to show you." She led the way down some steps, past a door with a sign that read Powder Magazine.

"Wait, what's this?" Nick asked, tapping on the black wooden door studded with nail heads. "Is it where the soldiers read magazines while they powdered their noses?"

Mandy snorted. "Haha, you're so funny. No, it's where they stored the gun powder."

"Oh, cool. Let's take a look. I want to see the gunpowder."

"There's none there—it's just an empty room. Come on."

Right next to the Powder Magazine a door stood open. Above it a sign announced Officers' Quarters.

Inside, their footsteps echoed on the wooden floor made of long, dusty planks as they walked through a doorway into a bigger room. A tall, black metal fence boxed off an area that contained a display of antique stuff and a mannequin dressed like a Civil War officer sitting at a desk. A wooden bed frame at the other end held a lumpy mattress covered by a wool blanket.

"Hey, cool," Nick said, studying the display. An oil lamp, metal dishes and a big jug stood on a wooden table in front of a brick fireplace. *That's all they had for heat?* Nick thought. *It must have been awful cold in here in the winter.* At least the windows were real glass instead of just holes in the wall. A washboard and tub sat by a window. *If that's how they washed their clothes, they probably didn't do it often. And that pitcher and basin on the stand must have been all they had to wash themselves. Who would want to take their clothes off to do that? Brrr. So they were probably pretty smelly guys.* Mandy had told him the regular soldiers during the Spanish-American War lived in tents outside on the grassy slopes. So the officers had it better with beds to sleep in, even if they were lumpy, and with some heat, even though it wouldn't be that warm. He shivered. Even in July, it was cold in the barracks.

Slow footsteps made the floor boards over their heads creak.

Nick snapped out of his thoughts of the past. "I thought your aunt said we were the only ones here," he said. "Someone's up there." He pointed at the ceiling.

Mandy glanced up. "The fort doesn't open for another half hour. Maybe it's her. "Aunt Julie, is that you?" she called.

No one answered. The footsteps stopped. A trickle of dust sifted down between the floor boards.

Nick stared at Mandy. "Who do you think it is?"

"Let's go see," she murmured. Mandy led him outside and jogged down to another open doorway where wooden stairs led up to the level above. She looked over her shoulder at him and put a finger to her lips.

Their rubber-soled sneakers made little sound as they climbed the stairs. When they reached the top, they stared in the direction the footsteps had come from, but couldn't see much of the next room.

"This way," Mandy whispered. They tiptoed to the doorway in the left wall, trying to keep the floorboards from squeaking.

They peeked into the next room. Empty. Another doorway led into the room that had been above them when they heard the footsteps. They shuffled in, looking around. Tarps hung here and there, making temporary walls where spooks would be located on Fright Night. Already, a dummy hung from a scaffold, a noose pulled tight around his neck.

"Maybe he's hiding," Mandy said in a low voice.

As Nick stared at the bulging eyes of the life-like dummy, he caught movement out of the corner of his eye. He spun around just in time to see the dark shape of someone disappearing through another doorway. "There he goes!"

They raced after the mysterious figure. They clattered down stone stairs and stopped. To the left lay the casemate area and in front of them another staircase led down to an outside door.

"Which way should we go?" Nick asked. *How could someone disappear so fast?*

"I'll check the casemates, you go down to the dry moat!" Mandy said.

Nick hurried down the steps and out into the sunshine. At the end of a brick walkway which bordered a grassy area between two long walls˙of the fort, another door stood open. He rushed inside. "Whoa," he said. Some daylight filtered through rifle slots in the wall, but it was still pretty dark. The tunnel seemed to go on forever. Nick gulped and snapped on his mini light. The beam didn't penetrate far, just enough to guide his footsteps. He walked a few yards and his feet slowed. He really didn't want to go any farther down the creepy tunnel. Besides, if there was someone there, he would hear him. Wouldn't he? The intruder must have gone the other way. Nick headed back to find Mandy. He could see her following the edge of the parade grounds, checking in each of the casemates.

When she spotted him, she trotted over. "Any luck?"

"I didn't see anyone," he replied.

"There are a million places to hide. But why would a person run away from us?" Mandy asked, puzzled.

Their eyes locked. "There's only one reason I can think of for someone to be sneaking around," said Nick. "He didn't want to be seen. "

Mandy's eyes widened in alarm. "That means he's up to something! We better go tell Aunt Julie."

## Chapter 2.   A Ghostly Figure

They found Mandy's aunt in the Visitors' Center.

"You saw someone walking around?" she asked them. "No one has come in since I unlocked the gate for you."

"We didn't actually see anyone—just heard footsteps over our heads in the Officers' Quarters," Mandy said. "We ran upstairs but no one was there."

"But I saw someone going into the doorway to the casemates," Nick added. "I couldn't see any details—just a dark shape."

"Hmmm," said Aunt Julie. She looked off for a moment, thinking. "I've seen the same thing myself a few times, but it's usually at dusk when I'm making the rounds before locking up."

"You have?" Nick said in surprise. "Who is it?"

"I don't know for sure," she said, "but my guess is old Sergeant Hegyi making *his* rounds. He was the caretaker here in the late 1800s. In fact, he died here."

"What?" Nick squawked. "Are you saying it was a-a-*ghost*?"

Mandy's brown eyes sparkled. "Aunt Julie, you didn't tell me Fort Knox is haunted! Wow, that makes it an even more interesting. Doesn't it, Nick?"

Nick moaned. "Interesting. . . right." *Great*, he thought, *another ghost. Just what we need.*

Aunt Julie winked at Mandy. "I've heard about your adventures from your dad. It sounds to me like you and Nick are extra sensitive to paranormal activity."

"What does that mean?" Nick asked, puzzled.

Mandy grinned. "It means we're ghost magnets, Nick."

He groaned again. "You got *that* right—unfortunately."

"Since you'll be staying with me for a week," Aunt Julie said, "you'll still be around after the first Summer Fright Night. The East Coast Ghost Trackers are coming in the following evening. They've been here before and found several 'hot spots' in the fort, including the second floor of the Officers' Quarters. I'll see if I can get you in, if you like. It's quite fascinating —they have all the gadgets for ghost-hunting— K2 sensors, infrared meters, audio enhancers, night vision scopes."

As she listed the devices, Nick perked up. Maybe it *would* be interesting, after all. He loved fooling around with cool gadgets. "Sure, I'll give it a try."

"All right!" said Mandy. "We're in!"

"Great," said Aunt Julie. "I'll see what I can do. Now, we still have fifteen minutes before the fort opens to the public. I'm going to take a look-see, just in case what you heard is a real person sneaking around. This Fright at the Fort event has caused some controversy. Some people think it's terrible that the fort is being used for something so tacky. Or to put it in loftier terms, 'the reputation of this sacred historical site should not be tarnished by ghouls and fools.'"

Nick glanced at Mandy. That sounded like *her* attitude about the fort.

Mandy frowned. "I can understand people feeling that way," she said. "But Fright Night brings in a lot of money that helps keep the fort in good shape. That's important too."

"You're right," said Aunt Julie. "And I bet it also brings in a lot of people who wouldn't normally visit the fort. So they get some history with their entertainment. Anyway, keep on the lookout today for anything suspicious. It's a big place and I can't be everywhere at once. You can be my extra eyes."

"Sure, Aunt Julie, we will," Mandy said. "Come on, Nick, let's check out Two-Step Alley."

"Another hot spot," her aunt said over her shoulder, as she dashed out the door.

A shiver rippled down Nick's spine. "I have a better idea. Let's go up to the roof now. You promised and I want to see the awesome view."

"Oh, all right," his cousin agreed. "We have plenty of time to look around—like all week. Let's go."

From the Visitors' Center, they made their way back to the main entrance of the fort. The tall black metal gates were open.

"Aunt Julie must have decided to unlock the fort. There will be lots of people around soon," said Mandy, squinting at what looked like an angel with a skull face hanging from one gate. "What's that supposed to be anyway?"

"Must be a ghoul," Nick said, snickering, "and there's the fool." He pointed at a skeleton sitting in a green canoe next to the wall. "He lost his paddle."

Mandy grinned. "And got left high and dry."

They went back inside and made their way to the other tower in the corner of the courtyard.

"Come on," said Nick. He couldn't *wait* to get to the top. He clambered up the steps with Mandy right behind him.

As they came out into the daylight, Nick shielded his eyes against the sudden brightness. The roof of the fort was a big stretch of grass broken up by low granite platforms that once held cannons. He would have liked to have seen it with all the cannons in place, but he could imagine what it must have been like. An American flag fluttered atop a flagpole in a part of the fort that jutted out. If he remembered right, it was called a bastion.

As Nick headed in that direction, he could see the wide river sparkling below and the sunlit buildings of Bucksport on the other side. To the left, the big paper mill, closed now and partially torn down, stood silent, its tall smokestacks pointing to the cloudless sky. Nick glanced to the right and then whistled in amazement. The Penobscot Narrows Bridge, a huge bridge with cables running down from two tall towers, spanned the river. They rode across it in Aunt Julie's car earlier that morning and it was *really* high. He looked forward to taking the elevator up to the observation deck in one of the towers. They planned to do that on the weekend after his family arrived from Nevada.

Mandy, who had seen it all many times, stood next to the safety railing that edged the open center of the roof and looked down to the parade grounds below. "Nick!" she said. "Come quick!"

"What is it?" he asked.

She just waved her arm wildly at him.

"What now?" he muttered, but he trotted over to her.

"Look!" she said in a low voice, pointing to the side of the parade grounds opposite the casemates.

Someone seemed to be skulking down a narrow, below ground-level walkway that ran beside the long wall. They could just see a bobbing head, wearing a dark brimmed hat.

"Is that the ghost of old Sergeant Hegyi?" Nick asked his cousin, hoping she would laugh it off. No such luck.

"Let's go find out," said Mandy.

## Chapter 3. Doors to Nowhere

"What's down here?" Nick asked, as they descended the steps to the below-ground walkway.

"The vaults," Mandy replied.

"Vaults?" Nick repeated, stopping in his tracks. "As in tombs? Where they put dead bodies? Where Dracula hangs out?"

"No, silly," she said. "*Storage* vaults— where they stored food and supplies."

Nick was disappointed and relieved at the same time. At the first opening, he snapped on his flashlight and fanned it across the interior of an arched, brick-lined space. Fallen bricks littered the dirt floor. The air seemed damp and musty. It would actually make a perfect tomb. But it contained no dead bodies, real or fake. He shivered. "No one in here." He backed out of the opening.

The next six vaults looked the same, except that one had a circular grate in the ceiling. Daylight streamed through it, creating a cool pattern of dark and light lines on the wall. All the rooms were empty, with nothing to hide behind.

They trudged up a stairway at the end of the walkway and stood in another corner of the parade grounds.

"Now what?" asked Nick. "He could have gone anywhere." He eyes scanned the outside of the wall that had been above them as they travelled through the below-ground walkway. It was long, stretching down the entire length of the courtyard with two floors of 12-paned glass windows in white-painted frames. The expanse of windows was interrupted by several white doors in the middle of the wall, two above and two below. He pointed at the second-story doors, which would have opened onto nothing but air. "Isn't that dangerous? Doors to nowhere? Hopefully, there are signs inside that warn, 'Watch that first step!'"

Mandy smirked at him. "Funny, Nick. Come on, let's take a look."

They headed up another set of steps with a sign with Enlisted Men's Quarters over the doorway.

Inside they found a big wooden box on legs beside a long wooden shelf with a sign that said Kneading Table. Behind it a brick wall contained open iron doors of different sizes, some just big enough for a person to crawl into.

"This is the bakery," Mandy said.

"Reminds me of Hansel and Gretel," Nick commented. "The witch in the gingerbread house would have loved this oven. She could have baked a dozen kids at the same time!"

"Right, Nick," Mandy said, rolling her eyes. "Aunt Julie said they actually never used the ovens. They set up field kitchens to make bread for the soldiers. Aunt Julie said when troops were here during the Spanish-American War, it took 400 loaves of bread a day to feed them all."

"Heh, heh, that's a lot of dough,' said Nick. "Your turn, Mandy, to take a look. Just peek into the ovens and make sure Sergeant Hegyi isn't baking muffins."

Mandy snorted and shined her light into one of the dark holes. "Well, silly, he wouldn't be *in* the oven."

"With ghosts you never know. They can be anywhere." To the right of the ovens, he found a narrow passageway that slotted in between two brick walls with a low granite lintel overhead. His flashlight illuminated it for a few yards and then it twisted out of sight. Beyond the entrance, the walls became stone, almost like it had been chiseled out of the bedrock. The floor was hard-packed earth. It reminded him of the tunnels in the ghost mine in Nevada near where he lived— the *haunted* mine. "Where do you think this goes?" Nick asked. He wasn't about to find out. Who knew what might be around that corner?

His cousin joined him and peered in. "Let's follow it."

"Uh, you go ahead. Ladies first," Nick said. "Plus you're smaller than me. I don't want to get stuck."

"Yeah, right," she said, starting into the passageway.

In a moment, she disappeared around the bend, but Nick could still see the glow of her light. "What do you see?" he called.

No answer.

"Mandy?"

Her light vanished.

"Mandy, answer me!"

Shoot, he *really* didn't want to go in there. Did she fall into a trap? Trip and knock herself out? Get kidnapped by the ghost? He supposed he had to rescue her. Nick took a deep breath, gathering his courage. He took a few steps into the tunnel. . . and then a few more. He had reached the bend and couldn't see beyond it. "Mandy?" he said again.

"Ooooo," wailed an unearthly voice.

Nick froze. The hairs on the back of his neck stood up. "M-Mandy?" Was she trying to scare him? "Cut it out," he said, hoping it was her.

Mandy sidled out of the narrow tunnel, her light catching Nick full in the face. He raised an arm and cringed away from her.

"What are you doing?" he yelled. "That was a mean trick!"

"Go!" she said, pushing him out of the passageway.

Back in the oven room, he scowled at her in anger. Then he noticed her white face. "What's the matter?" he demanded.

"I didn't try to scare you, Nick," Mandy said.

"But. . ."

"It wasn't me. I heard it too."

Nick shivered. "Where did the tunnel go?"

"Dead end. It curves behind the oven and stops."

"Great," muttered Nick. "If it wasn't you, it was someone—or something—else!"

"That's a logical deduction, Sherlock. Come on. Let's look in the Enlisted Men's Quarters—maybe the sound came from there."

The first room branched off from the bakery, an arched brick space with a plank floor. The heavy wooden frame of a bunk bed stood against the end wall, the only object in the room.

After that, a series of rooms connected to each other by a few stone steps. They differed from the first room because they had loose dirt floors and were totally empty. The sandy floors reminded Nick of a big ash tray. It must have been hard for the enlisted men to keep their shoes shiny.

"It's strange how each room is higher than the last," Mandy said.

"Well," Nick said, "I looked at some old pictures in the Visitors' Center. "When they built the fort, they had to fit it into the hillside that's here. Because they wanted the parade grounds in the center to be level, the sections around it had to rise up one after another like giant steps."

After traipsing through two rooms, they entered one with a door in its outside wall. Wide boards had been nailed across it to keep people from opening it.

"That's a relief," said Nick. "No one's going to fall out. But why do you think they put doors way up here?"

"Aunt Julie said they planned to build wooden barracks above the underground vaults. They would have connected to these rooms by wooden walkways. These were bombproof rooms for the soldiers if the fort was under attack."

"Why didn't the wooden barracks get built?" Nick asked, puzzled.

"After the Spanish-American War, the fort wasn't needed anymore," Mandy said in a sad voice, "so they didn't finish it. . .come on, let's go."

As they headed up the steps to the next room, Mandy stopped.

Nick bumped into her and almost fell. "Now what?" he demanded, catching his balance just in time.

"Shhh," she whispered. "Look!"

The open doorways leading into each room lined up with each other, allowing a long view. Way down near the end, Nick saw the silhouette of a person. Man or ghost? He couldn't tell.

"Come on!" Mandy said, taking off like a horse at the starting line. She raced through each room, taking the stairs at a gallop.

Nick took off after her. Breathing hard, he tried to keep up. That girl could run.

The dark figure seemed to turn and look their way and then started running too.

When Nick and Mandy reached the end of the line, panting for breath, they faced another dead end.

"This is the cistern room," said Mandy, "where the drinking water was stored." She climbed up on a wooden step stool and tried to peer over the wall into the cistern, but she was too short. "There's no other way out."

Nick, who was taller, shimmied up onto the wall and shined his light in the cistern. Empty. "Where—did he—go?" he asked between gasps.

## Chapter 4. An Army of Shadows

"How could someone just vanish?" Nick asked, looking around the small, empty room.

"Well, a *someone* couldn't," said Mandy, "but a ghost could. Maybe Sergeant Hegyi is playing hide-and-seek with us. Anyway, we'll never find him now. The tourists have arrived." She pointed out the window at several people who strolled across the courtyard, stopping now and then to take a photo.

"This place is creepy," said Nick. "Maybe we just *thought* we saw something—you know, a trick of the light? And maybe the wailing sound was the wind or something." He didn't really believe that, but he didn't want to think about it anymore. "Besides, I'm hungry. Let's go see if there's anything to eat in the Visitors' Center."

"There *was* someone there," Mandy insisted. "Don't you want to look around more?"

"Sure, but not right now. As you said, we've got all week. My stomach's growling."

Mandy sighed. "You're *always* hungry."

"Hey," Nick protested, "I'm a growing boy. I need to keep up my strength."

She snorted. "What strength?"

"My point exactly," he said, grinning.

Back at the Visitors' Center, Aunt Julie was nowhere to be seen.

"She's out giving a tour," said the tall young woman behind the counter, who happened to be Julie's daughter, Brooke. She brushed back her dark hair cut in a short, sassy style and winked at them. "She said if you stopped in, to give you the trail mix and fruit juice in the back room. Come on in." She gestured for them to step behind the counter and into the Friends of Fort Knox office.

"Do you have Peyton with you?" Mandy asked. She adored Brooke's feisty, fun eight-year-old daughter.

"Not today. She's with her babysitter." She chuckled. "I thought I'd give the tourists a break from watching her gymnastic routines. But she's hoping to hang out with you soon. You are her favorite cousin—or technically, second cousin. She loves you to pieces, Mandy."

Mandy smiled. "I can't wait to see her. Oh, and this is my cousin Nick from Nevada. I don't think you've met."

"Hi, Nick." Brooke's pretty face became serious. "Mom said you saw someone prowling around earlier?"

Nick jumped in. "Yeah, we caught a glimpse of someone, but couldn't see any details. We just saw him again in the Enlisted Men's Quarters, way down near the last room. He vanished into thin air. We still don't know if it's a real person or the ghost of Sergeant Hegyi."

"Ah," said Brooke, hiding a smile with her hand, "Mom told you about him. I've never seen a ghost here, so I tend to think it's a real person —which is actually more of a worry than a ghost." She grew serious again. "There have been some strange things happening."

"Like what?" Nick asked.

"Well, you know we're getting ready for the first summer Fright at the Fort?" When they nodded, she continued. "The volunteers who are setting things up are finding props out of place and even some things broken. It's as if someone is trying to undo everything we prepare. It's frustrating. The money these events bring in is really important for the upkeep of the fort."

Aunt Julie came through the door in time to hear the last of her daughter's comments. "You're not kidding that it's frustrating. As I led a group through the upstairs Officers' Quarters, I discovered the strobe light machine had been bashed with a brick. Pieces of it are all over the floor. I'm sure it's ruined." Her shoulders slumped. "The destruction seems to be escalating. Maybe we'll have to cancel Fright Night."

"Oh, no, Aunt Julie," Mandy said, "you can't do that! We'll help, won't we, Nick?"

"Sure," Nick replied, "but we can't be everywhere at once. This guy is sneaky. . . and he moves fast." He stopped for a minute. "Do you think it's just one person or maybe more?"

Aunt Julie groaned. "What an awful thought—a team of fanatics set on sabotage? How do we fight that?"

"I have an idea," said Mandy. "Nick, didn't you bring your walkie-talkies with you?"

"Yeah, I left them in the car. I thought it would be fun to use them later. First, I just wanted to get a look at the fort. What are you thinking?"

"If we split up and patrol the areas where the main equipment for Fright Night is located, we can keep a better eye on things and still be able to communicate with the walkie-talkies."

"Good idea, Mandy," said Aunt Julie, looking more hopeful. "Most of the props are in the casemates, on the second floor of the Officers' Quarters and in the rooms beside where the ammo is stored."

"Ammo?" Nick asked, his ears perking up. "How did I miss that?"

"We never made it all the way around the edge of the courtyard," said Mandy. "The Ordnance Storeroom is one of the rooms between the Enlisted Men's Quarters and the gate we came in."

Nick's eyes sparkled. "I wouldn't mind hanging out there."

Brooke chuckled. "Yes, protect the gunpowder at all costs. We don't want the fort blown up." Then she frowned. "They wouldn't really do that, would they?"

Her mother shook her head. "My guess is whoever is doing this is just trying to sabotage Fright at the Fort. They don't want to harm the fort itself. . .I hope. And of course, there isn't really gunpowder in the kegs. They're just made to look real."

Mandy had a thought. "Brooke, could Peyton come with you to work tomorrow? She could help us patrol."

Brooke frowned. "I'm not sure if she would be a help or a hindrance. What do you think, Mom?"

"I think the more we have helping, the better. She's a pretty observant child. She needs to stay close to you though, Mandy. I don't want her wandering around alone."

"Sure thing. It will be fun to hang out together."

"So for now, if you could keep an eye on the areas I mentioned, it will help. I doubt if someone would try to destroy things when visitors are around, but you never know. I've got to figure out how this idiot—or gang of idiots— is getting in before the fort opens." Aunt Julie shook her head. "Two more days to get through. I'll be so glad when Fright Night is behind us. . .if there's anything left by then. It's like fighting an army of shadows."

"We'll do our best to help," Mandy said.

"We sure will," agreed Nick. "We're up for the battle. Let's go get the walkie-talkies and start patrolling."

## Chapter 5.  A Dedicated Soldier

"That was fun this afternoon," Nick said at dinner that evening. "It felt like we were on a special mission."

"We *were* on a special mission," said Mandy, "protecting the fort from intruders. What could be more important than that?" She took a bite of her taco.

"I really appreciate you two keeping an eye on the Fright Night equipment," Aunt Julie said. "I'm glad you didn't find it boring, even though nothing happened. The thing is, if anyone *was* set on sabotage, just your presence would make them think twice. . .and the walkie-talkies are a great idea, Nick. People don't know who you are talking to on them—it could be a direct line to the police." She set a refilled bowl of salsa on the kitchen table.

"These tacos are delicious, Aunt Julie," Mandy said. "Thanks so much for making them for us."

"No problem. Dessert will be even better."

That caught Nick's attention. "Dessert? What is it?"

"We're going to walk to the ice cream take-out on Main Street. My treat. They have flavors unique to Maine like Wild Blueberry, Lobster Tracks, Muddy Boots, Fly Fishing Fudge, Moose Tracks. "

"Sounds interesting," Nick said. "Do they have Deer Droppings or maybe Rabbit Pellets?"

Mandy gagged on her taco. "Don't be disgusting, Nick." She looked at him cross-eyed and then changed the subject. "So, Aunt Julie, can you tell us more about Sergeant Hegyi? You said you think you've seen his ghost?"

"Well, I'm often the one who locks up at night. We close at sunset, so by the time I've had a look around the fort, it's getting dark. I don't know how many times I've caught a glimpse of someone down a long corridor and thought it was a visitor. But when I call out, the person vanishes."

"That's kind of creepy," Nick said, a cold shiver running down his back.

"So Sergeant Hegyi was once a caretaker at the fort?" Mandy said.

Aunt Julie nodded. "Yes, back in the 1800s. His first name was Leopold and he was from Hungary. He came to America in 1849 and joined the army. He must have worked with horses in the Old Country because he became the horse trainer for Custer's troops in St. Louis, Missouri. You've heard of Custer's Last Stand, haven't you?"

"Sure," Nick said. "General Custer got defeated by the Indians at Little Big Horn. It was pretty much a massacre."

"Well, the horses those soldiers rode into the battle were probably trained by Sergeant Hegyi. He got reassigned to be caretaker of Fort Knox in 1883."

"How long did he take care of the fort?" Mandy asked.

"For thirteen years," Aunt Julie replied. "When the Connecticut troops manned the fort during the Spanish-American War, Sergeant Hegyi was the 'go-to man'. He knew everything about the fort. But they only stayed a few months. After they left, he was all alone again. He walked down to the Prospect store at the wharf landing each evening to socialize a little and then headed back up the hill to his small house by the fort. He got sick and died in 1900."

"Is he buried at the fort?" Nick asked, trying to remember if he had seen a graveyard—other than the fake one by the main entrance.

"No, his grave is in the Narrows Cemetery about a mile up the road."

"So why do you think his ghost might be haunting the fort?" Mandy asked. "It wasn't a violent death."

Aunt Julie shrugged. "It's just a guess. The fort was everything to him. It makes sense that his spirit would be attracted to a place he held so dear. . .or maybe he has unfinished business that's keeping him from resting in peace."

"Hmm," said Mandy, "I wonder what it might be? Did he have any family?"

"Yes, his wife lived in New York. She was notified that he was very ill, but by the time she arrived, Sergeant Hegyi had died."

"Oh, that's sad," Mandy said. "I wonder why they lived so far apart?"

"No one knows. Maybe she didn't want to leave New York. To her, Maine might have seemed like the ends of the earth."

"Or maybe they didn't get along that well," Nick suggested. "Anyway, so when are we taking that walk for ice cream? I left just enough room." He patted his stomach.

Aunt Julie laughed. "Let's just clear the table first and then we'll go. We're meeting Brooke and Peyton there. I'll give them a call."

At the take-out, they ordered cones and then sat on the long stone bench set back from the sidewalk under a big maple tree.

"Moose Tracks is awesome," Nick said, taking one of the tiny peanut butter cups into his mouth and biting down on it for some intense flavor. "But I still think Deer Droppings would be a winner."

Peyton giggled. She perched between Mandy and Nick, enjoying her blue Smurf cone. "Yeah, they could put little malted milk balls in vanilla ice cream. Pretty tasty."

Nick grinned over her head at Mandy, glad to have found someone who appreciated his humor. He liked this kid with her blonde pig tails and big brown eyes. No doubt she would get along great with his sister Christianne. His family planned to fly in on Saturday from Nevada in time for the big family reunion on Sunday. He was so lucky they had let him come to Maine early to spend a week with Mandy and her aunt.

From where they sat, they could see the Penobscot Narrows Bridge and Fort Knox, both lit up against the darkening sky.

"Nice view," Nick commented. "From here, you can really see how well situated the fort is to fight off invaders coming up the river."

"And you can see how well designed it is to fit into the hillside," Mandy added. She licked the last of her Mint Chocolate Chip out of the tiny cone that remained and then crunched that up. "Yum, that was good." She gave a contented sigh.

"I wouldn't mind coming here every day so we could try out all the flavors," Nick said. "I might go for Campfire S'mores next." Out of the corner of his eye, a movement distracted him, and he looked straight at the fort again. "Uh, Julie? Brooke? There's someone over at the fort. Look!"

They all stared across the water. A pinprick of light wavered near the main gate.

"Well, it can't be Sergeant Hegyi this time," said Aunt Julie in a grim voice. "Ghosts don't need a flashlight to see. Whoever it is, he's outside the walls. With all that's been going on, it makes me nervous. I want to go over and check it out. Brooke, can you look after the kids?"

"Mom, no way are you going alone. It's not safe. We'll all go. We can take my car." She pointed to the silver SUV parked across the street. "Come on."

They hurried to the crosswalk and piled into Brooke's vehicle.

"Fasten your seatbelts," she said to the kids over her shoulder. "Here we go."

*Is it the intruder?* Nick wondered. *What will we find at the fort?*

## Chapter 6. The Intruder

"Don't let the car doors slam," Julie said, as they pulled into the Fort Knox parking lot. "Whoever's here, we don't want them to hear us coming."

They jumped out of Brooke's SUV and eased the doors shut.

A glint of something shiny farther down the lot caught Nick's eye. "Hey, over there," he said in a low voice, "it's a motorcycle."

"I'll take a look," said Aunt Julie. "The fort closes at sunset, so that bike shouldn't be here. The parking lot gate is closed. The rider must have squeezed in between the posts in the old entrance."

"Be careful, Mom," Brooke warned. "Someone might be nearby."

"I'll protect you, Gram!" Peyton said.

Nick chuckled. This kid tickled his funny bone. He could just picture her with hands on hips, scolding the intruder for being so bad. She was feisty enough.

"We'll all stay together," Brooke said, taking her daughter's hand to keep her from rushing ahead.

"Does anyone have a flashlight?" Aunt Julie asked. "The power's low in my phone. I don't want to waste it using the light in case I need to call the police."

"I've got mine." Brooke put her hand in her jacket pocket, but it came out empty. "Shoot, it's in my other jacket. I changed just before we left for the take-out."

"I've got a light," said Mandy, digging her mini light out of her pocket. "Always be prepared, that's my motto!" She handed it to her aunt.

Aunt Julie snapped it on and led the way across the parking lot. She aimed it at a mud-splattered dirt bike. "Hmm, no telling who owns this. We'll go around to the front of the fort. Keep together and stay quiet." She jogged back across the lot and down past the Visitors' Center.

The tacos and ice cream in Nick's stomach sloshed around as he trotted after the rest of the group. He moaned. Was he the only one that felt like barfing?

At the main gate, they stopped. There was no one in sight.

Nick leaned against the wall, gasping and holding his stomach.

"No sense in checking outside," Aunt Julie said in a low voice. "We'll go see if anyone is inside." She focused the light on the gate's padlock. "The gate's still locked." She used her key and undid the chain. Her soft-soled shoes barely made a sound on the cobblestone passage as she walked past the ghoul in the canoe and up to the edge of the inner courtyard. "Use your eyes and ears, but not your voices," she whispered. She snapped off the light.

As his eyes got used to the dark, Nick noticed he could see the center of the parade grounds clearly, but inky pools of shadow surrounded it. He shivered. The fort looked sinister at night. *Anything* could come out of those caverns of blackness. Was he really up to Fright Night? The thought of a gruesome figure stepping out of the dark with a bloody ax made chills run down his arms.

Mandy tapped him on the shoulder and he almost screamed. The sound came out as a muffled grunt. She stuck her face in front of his with a finger to her lips and nodded toward the far end of the courtyard. He noticed everyone else staring in that direction.

On the second floor of the Officer's Quarters, a light moved in front of a window.

Nick gulped. Someone—or some*thing*—was there. Maybe it was the ghost of old Sergeant Hegyi checking things out. *Would a ghost need a light?* Probably not. So it had to be a real person. . .which might be even scarier than a pretend zombie or ax murderer.

"Stay here," Aunt Julie whispered, "and keep your eyes peeled. If anyone runs this way, yell!"

"Can I come with you, Gram?" Peyton asked in a small, brave voice.

"No, Sweetie, I need you to stay here and watch for the bad guys."

The little girl nodded and stood up taller. "Okay."

"Mom, please be careful," Brooke pleaded. "Don't do anything foolish."

"I'll be fine." Stepping up into the casemates so she wouldn't be seen approaching the Officers' Quarters, Aunt Julie disappeared into the darkness.

Nick could imagine her making her way from one casemate to the next, climbing the stone steps in between each level, passing the big cannon and finally reaching the farthest casemate in the corner of the courtyard. Up the staircase she would go, stepping out onto the second floor where he could still see the light moving around. Wasn't that dangerous? Confronting a person face-to-face who wasn't supposed to be there? He could feel his hands sweating in the cool evening air.

The sound of splintering wood shattered the silence.

"Good grief, what's that?" Mandy said.

They heard a muffled shout. Another light joined the first, the two beams waving around like a battle of light sabers.

"Oh, shoot!" said Brooke. "I've got to go help her! Stay hidden, guys!" She herded them behind the stone pillar of a casemate and then raced along the edge of the parade grounds, not caring if anyone saw her.

"Mom!" Peyton called after her.

"Peyton, stay with us," Mandy said, grabbing the girl's arm before she could follow Brooke. "We need to stand guard."

As the children peered out from the darkness of the casemate, they heard more shouting.

"Something's going on," Nick said. "Maybe we should go help too."

"I don't know—they told us to stay here," replied Mandy.

Nick could hear the indecision in her voice. He knew she hated missing out on the action as much as he did—maybe more.

"I want to help Mom and Gram!" Peyton said with no hesitation. She jumped off the edge of the casemate and started running toward the voices.

"Wait, Peyton!" Mandy called.

She and Nick both took off after her. When they were halfway along the courtyard, a dark figure darted out of the far doorway of the Officers' Quarters and headed down the other side.

Remembering what Brooke had said, Nick stopped and yelled, "Hey, you, hold it right there!"

A head turned his way, and then the figure continued at an even faster pace.

"What should we do?" Nick asked, glancing around for Mandy.

She and Peyton had already disappeared into the end casemate.

Nick groaned. "What should *I* do?" Follow the girls or chase the bad guy? He knew it would be safer to stay with the crowd. But if he followed the intruder, he might discover how he was getting in.

As he stood rooted to the spot, undecided, the dark figure sped across the courtyard, headed for the main gate. The intruder was getting away.

"Rats," Nick muttered. He jogged across the grass. When he got to the stone archway of the main gate, he stopped and peered around the edge of the wall. He caught a glimpse of movement and for a moment, the silhouette of the fleeing figure stood out against the lights of Bucksport. Nick trotted after him. Just as he cleared the gate, he saw the man duck into the doorway of a small white building way off to the left. Just great. If Nick followed him in there, he'd get conked on the head for sure. He wished he had a flashlight. Why wasn't he 'always prepared' like Mandy? He hadn't thought he'd need one to go to the ice cream place.

As Nick got closer, the opening of the building, a yawning black hole, beckoned to him. He wiped beads of sweat off his forehead. He picked up a couple of rocks and walked to the doorway. He tossed one in. It sounded like it bounced against stones, gradually fading away. A long stairway going down? Where did it go?

## Chapter 7. Destruction

Nick took a deep breath and stepped into the dark doorway. He almost fell and grabbed the door frame just in time. The stairs started right away with no landing first. He clenched the spare rock in his hand, ready to use it as a weapon if the intruder attacked. Right off, though, he knew he was alone. Down below on what must be a ver-r-ry long staircase, he could hear footsteps. The intruder, who obviously knew his way around better than Nick did, was escaping. Nick wondered where the stairs led. Too bad he and Mandy had wasted the afternoon guarding the inside of the fort. They never had a chance to look around outside the walls.

No way would Nick try to follow him without a light—maybe not even *with* a light. Too dangerous. He might as well go find the others. He stepped out of the small building and headed back to the main gate. Before going inside, he gazed down the hillside toward the river. Off to the left, he thought he saw a glimmer of light for a moment. Was it the intruder? Could the stairs have come out way down there? This place was like a huge maze. Tomorrow he would check out the grounds to get a better idea of the layout. As he stood there hoping for another glimpse of the light, he heard the sound of a boat motor starting.

"That's strange," he muttered. He knew sound carried quite far across water, but could he really hear a motorboat all the way from Bucksport? He shrugged. Maybe a fisherman was late getting home.

Nick trudged through the gate and across the courtyard. A light still wavered on the second floor of the Officers' Quarters. He ducked into the last casemate and felt his way up the steps in the dark. He peeked into the upper room.

In the faint beam of Mandy's flashlight, he could see Julie, Brooke and the girls gathered round a wooden contraption that lay splintered on the floor. He also spotted a noose wrapped around the neck of a dummy. Oh, yeah, the make-believe gallows. The sight of that thing hanging limply from the rope gave him the chills when he saw it earlier in the day.

"It's me," Nick said to warn them he was there.

"Hey, Nick," said Mandy. "Did you see the guy who did this?"

"Just his silhouette," Nick replied, "as he ran out the gate. I followed him to that little white house off to the left."

"I bet he took the stairs to Battery B," Julie said.

"Huh?" Nick said, confused. "What battery?"

"It's a military term," explained Brooke. "The planners of the fort intended to position a group of cannons down by the riverbank—that's called a battery. There's another stairway to the right of the main gate that leads down to Battery A. Both have what's called a hot shot furnace where the cannonballs could be heated up. When fired, that type of cannonball could set a wooden ship on fire."

"Cool," said Nick.

"If the intruder went down to Battery B, he could be anywhere by now," Aunt Julie said. She sighed. "This is getting out of control. I'm worried someone will get hurt."

"Did you get a look at his face?" Nick asked.

"He had a black ski mask on," she replied. "He must have knocked over the gallows and then when I saw him, he was whacking it apart with a hammer. I yelled but he dropped the hammer and ran."

"How about fingerprints?" Mandy asked, crouching near the hammer where it lay on the floor.

"He wore gloves."

"Were you scared, Gram?" Peyton asked, taking her hand.

"No, but I sure was mad. . .and still am."

"I think I can fix this," said Nick. "It doesn't look too broken up." He surveyed the pile of boards that had once been a scaffold. "If you have an extra board and a few nails I can patch this cracked one."

Julie sighed again. "Thanks, Nick. Sure, you kids can do that in the morning before you start patrolling. That would be a big help. The question is: What will be wrecked next?"

Mandy's face scrunched in thought. "We need more guards," she said. "Could you get some volunteers who would help out with keeping watch?"

"Maybe we could," Brooke said. "The only problem is we don't know who we can trust. What if someone volunteers who is actually out to make trouble?"

"Whoa, that's a good point, Brooke," said her mother. "What if we already have a volunteer who's causing trouble? The people setting up the Fright Night props have unlimited access here, at least during regular hours."

"But someone, like this intruder, is getting in a different way," said Nick. "It shouldn't be that hard to find."

Mandy shook her head. "That's easy to say, Nick, but it's a really big place."

"Could they climb up the wall?" Peyton asked. "Like Spiderman?"

Nick chuckled. He liked the way her mind worked—a lot like his own. "That's not such a crazy idea," he said, giving her a fist bump. "What if someone had a ladder? Could they fit through a rifle slot?"

"It would have to be a really long ladder!" Mandy said. "How would they get it here?"

"Maybe we should take a look around outside," said Aunt Julie. "The guy left in a hurry so maybe he didn't have time to cover up his way in. Come on."

They trooped down the stairs and out the main gate.

"That's where I saw the light," Nick said, pointing down the hillside next to the river.

"Yes, that's Battery B," said Brooke. "By now he could have made his way back to the parking lot. Let's go see if the dirt bike is gone."

"Why didn't I think to get the license plate?" Aunt Julie said in frustration. "We could have had the police run it and find out who it belongs to."

"It's not your fault, Gram," Peyton said. "We were in a hurry to catch the bad guy *and* the license plate was really dirty."

They stopped at the Visitors' Center to pick up a more powerful flashlight. Aunt Julie handed the penlight back to Mandy. "Thanks, Mandy, you're a good girl scout. 'Always be prepared' is a good motto for all of us."

In the parking lot, they were surprised to see the dirt bike still there.

"Hmm," said Brooke. "This means either the bike doesn't belong to the intruder or he's still around." She took a tissue out of her pocket and wiped the dried mud off the license plate. "Anyway, it gives us a chance to find out who the owner is. Does anyone have paper and a pen?"

"I do!" said Peyton, pulling out a tiny puppy notebook and a miniature purple pen. "I'm a good girl scout too!"

"Yes, you are!" said Mandy. "Give me five!"

Brooke wrote down the license number while Julie held the light on it. "I'll keep watch here while you check the walls," Brooke said, "just in case he comes back."

"Stay hidden!" her mother warned. "And don't try to confront him. Promise?"

"Okay, okay," Brooke agreed. "I'll just try to get a good look at him."

Brooke hid behind a tree as Julie led the children off into the darkness.

## Chapter 8. On Patrol

"It's strange we didn't find anything last night," Mandy said, as they rode to the fort the next morning. "You would think the intruder would have left some clue as to how he got in."

"I'll check again now that it's daylight," Julie said. "We might have missed something in the dark."

"We'll go put the gallows back together and then start patrolling," Nick said, holding up the walkie-talkies.

When they walked down the path to the Visitors' Center, they could see Peyton doing cartwheels in front of the building.

She spotted them and waved. "Watch this!" The little girl ran and did a forward flip, landing on her feet. She grinned at them.

"Awesome," Nick said. "I wish I could do that."

"I'll teach you how!" Peyton offered.

"Uh, no, that's okay," Nick said, picturing himself falling flat on his back like a bumbling clown. "I'd probably hurt myself."

"Would you like to learn how to do a cartwheel instead?" Peyton looked at him with eager eyes.

Nick hated to disappoint her. "Maybe later," he said. *Like never,* he thought. "Right now we have work to do. Do you want to carry the nails?"

"Sure!" she said, taking the small bag. "I promise not to spill them."

Mandy carried the extra board they had brought from Aunt Julie's house and Nick toted the walkie-talkies.

"So we'll have to figure out who's going to patrol where," Nick said, as they walked through the main gate and along the parade grounds to the Officers' Quarters. "I vote for the ammo room—once I know where it is."

"There are actually lots of powder magazines," Mandy said, "spread out around the fort. There's too much territory to cover for you to stay in one room. There aren't any Fright Night props in those rooms anyway."

"Shoot," said Nick. "Well, I want to at least *see* them."

"Sure," Mandy said. "Later."

They climbed the stairs to the second floor. The smashed gallows and hammer lay on the floor where they had left them the night before. Nick began pounding boards back together. Peyton handed him a nail each time he asked for one.

Mandy prowled around, searching for any clues they might have missed in the dark. Something on the floor caught her eye. "Hey, what's this?" She crouched down to study the object. "Hmm, it's a necklace. Do you have a tissue, Nick? Unused?"

Nick stopped hammering and dug a Kleenex out of his jeans' pocket. "Do you need to blow your nose?"

Mandy rolled her eyes. "No, I'm just being careful in case there are fingerprints on this."

Her cousin frowned at her. "It could belong to anyone who's been through here—not necessarily the intruder."

"True," she replied. "On the other hand, it *could* be a clue. Look at this design." She held it out on the tissue.

From a broken chain hung a bronze medallion etched with a weird-looking eye inside a five-pointed star.

"Hmm, it's kind of interesting. The eye reminds me of ancient Egypt. I drew one like that on my Egyptian picture in fourth grade art class.

I think it's supposed to mean something, but I can't remember what."

Peyton stared at the object in Mandy's hand. "I've seen that before. When Mom took me for a walk along the waterfront in town, it was spray-painted under the bridge."

"Really? That's weird," said Mandy, "It could be important. I'll hold onto it for now." She wrapped it in the tissue and pushed it into the pocket of her hoodie.

"Can you help me for a minute?" Nick asked. "Hold this board up straight while I hammer it to the other one." He held out his hand, and Peyton dropped a nail into it. Nick whacked it into the wood and then stepped back to survey his handiwork. "Good as new. Okay, let's set it up."

The children raised the scaffold back into place.

Feeling a little creeped out, Nick picked up the dummy with the noose around its neck and hooked it onto the scaffold. Even though he knew it wasn't real, goosebumps crept along his arms. "This dude should find a new place to 'hang' out," Nick said, trying to make a joke of it.

Mandy groaned. "That's lame, Nick."

Peyton giggled. "Really. He should stop 'hanging' around and get to work."

Nick grinned at her. Yup, he liked this kid a lot.

"So we need to decide who's going to patrol where," Mandy said. "Why don't you stay here, Nick, to keep watch on the second floor. This area seems to be the main target of the intruder."

Nick scowled. "Gee, thanks."

"You've got the walkie-talkie. If anything happens, just call us, and we'll come running. Peyton and I will patrol the casemates and storage rooms."

"See you later, Nick," Peyton said, giving him a little wave as she followed Mandy to the stairs. "Look out for the ghost of Sergeant Hegyi!"

"Why did she have to say that?" Nick muttered. He didn't like being left alone in this place. With the girls gone, the quiet pressed in on him. He supposed patrolling meant walking back and forth. He picked up the walkie-talkie and clipped it to the band of his jeans. He headed to the doorway of the next room, his feet making a hollow, clumping sound. Great, he thought, an intruder would hear him coming a mile away. Nick tried to tiptoe to make his feet quieter. The next room was empty, but a doorway at the far end opened into another space. He sighed and headed that way.

A flight of stone stairs led up into another dark passage. He pulled out his mini-light and snapped it on. The beam revealed a wall ahead. The tunnel must bend to the right. Should he look around the corner? Common sense told him to turn back to the Officers' Quarters—he had been assigned that area to guard, not this dank, spooky place. But he might as well take a look. He peered around the corner.

The floor was level for a few yards and then took two steps down, over and over. "Hmm, this must be the infamous Two-Step Alley," Nick murmured, "the place Julie said was another ghost 'hotspot.'" The fort reminded him of a video game—a giant maze that he had to navigate, conquering obstacles and battling bad guys along the way to survive. The tunnel was a handy pathway for someone to secretly get around to different parts of the fort and pop up in unexpected places.

The patter of light footfalls woke him up. Someone else *was* in the tunnel. The flashlight, too weak to shine far, was useless. The rifle slots in the outer wall let in enough daylight, though, to reveal a figure dressed in dark clothes nimbly dashing down Two-Step Alley.

Nick pulled the walkie-talkie off his waistband and pushed the 'talk' button. "Mandy, come in, it's Nick." He kept his voice low.

No reply.

"Mandy, come in!" he said urgently, not caring now if the intruder heard him. "May Day! Someone's running down Two-Step Alley!"

Still no reply.

## Chapter 9.  A Warning

Nick groaned. The walkie-talkie didn't work in the tunnel. . .maybe because of the thick stone walls? What should he do? No way would he chase the intruder. Anyone capable of smashing the gallows and strobe light wouldn't hesitate to bash Nick on the head if he tried to stop him.

He hurried back to the Officers' Quarters. As soon as his feet thumped on the wooden floor, he ran to the nearest window, hoping for a clear line of communication. He pressed the 'talk' button on the walkie-talkie. "Mandy? Come in, Mandy!"

The walkie-talkie squawked. "What's up?" Mandy asked.

"I spotted the intruder," Nick said, "running down Two-Step Alley! The walkie-talkie didn't work in there. I'm back on the second floor of the Officers' Quarters. Where does the tunnel come out?"

"Behind the storerooms! We're in the casemate to the right of the gate. We'll try to head him off."

"Mandy! Be careful! Wait, I'll come down."

No answer. His cousin had already signed off.

"Rats!" Nick murmured. "That guy is dangerous. He might hurt them if they get in the way." He jogged through the rooms to the staircase that led down to the casemates. From there, he skittered down more steps to the parade grounds and sprinted across the grass.

He stopped by one of the towers that led to the roof, trying to catch his breath. Where were the girls? He grabbed the walkie-talkie. "Mandy, this is Nick. I'm in front of the storerooms. Where are you?"

After a long pause, her voice answered. "We're right around the corner at the entrance to Two-Step Alley. It's hopeless. A big crowd just came in. Stay right there and we'll join you."

"Okay, over and out." Nick clipped the walkie-talkie back to the waistband of his jeans. He felt both frustrated and relieved at the same time. The intruder had escaped again, but at least the girls hadn't met him face-to-face. No telling what might have happened. He studied the people around him while he waited. They all looked like regular tourists—a mother and father with two kids, a young couple holding hands, a man looking at a map of the fort. How could the intruder just disappear?

Mandy and Peyton walked up to Nick.

"We haven't seen anyone suspicious," Mandy said. "Are you sure it was the intruder?"

"Well, why would the guy run down the tunnel if he wasn't up to something?" reasoned Nick.

"Actually it's fun to run down Two-Step Alley," said Mandy. "You're not supposed to, but kids do it all the time."

"He was too tall to be a kid."

"Maybe it was a teenager," said Peyton. "Teenagers are just big kids, aren't they? They like to have fun too."

Nick nodded. He was almost a teenager himself. "Yeah, I guess you're right." He felt relieved. "I better get back to my post. I don't want to leave the Officers' Quarters unguarded for long."

"Okay, we'll see you at noon," Mandy said. "We're having lunch at the Visitors' Center."

"Mom made Italian sandwiches for us," Peyton announced, "and chocolate coconut cookies for dessert. Yum!"

"I could use one of those cookies right now," said Nick. "I'm feeling a little weak. I don't suppose we could take an energy break?"

Mandy crossed her arms. "You're *always* thinking about food. We have a job to do."

Nick sighed. "Yeah, okay, back to work. Let me know when it's time to eat." He walked across the parade grounds. When he reached the casemate that held the big cannon, its dark shape seemed to call to him. It wouldn't hurt to stop for a minute and take a look. He liked to imagine what it would have been like if the British *had* attacked the fort. With cannons like this in every casemate pounding away, not to mention the ones down near the water, a fleet of ships wouldn't have gotten far. If any Redcoats did manage to get ashore, they would have been mowed down by rifle fire.

He studied the neat mound of cannon balls. They looked really heavy. He wondered how the soldiers got them into the cannon. Nick slid into the space between the cannon and the opening in the outer wall the cannonball would have been shot through. He peered into the big gun. As he got out his light to take a better look, he noticed a man walking by. The man didn't even glance at the cannon. That's strange, thought Nick. You'd think a tourist would stop to look. He was dressed all in black and had a short pointed black beard. Even stranger was the fact the guy wore sunglasses. Maybe in the dim light he didn't even *see* the cannon. Nick shrugged. Too bad he missed one of the best things in the fort.

I better get back to patrolling, Nick thought. He glanced at his watch and sighed. Still an hour until lunch. He trudged through the remaining casemates and back up to the Officers' Quarters. He would rather be outside seeing the rest of the fort layout. Maybe they could take a look at lunch time. Keeping guard wasn't as much fun as he thought it would be. You stand around, watching and waiting, hoping something bad doesn't happen. Just like the soldiers, Nick thought. They did a lot of that.

He scuffed around the room, shining his light on the Fright Night props to make sure everything was okay. Most of them had tarps or sheets over them to keep them out of sight until the big event. Nick supposed he should look under the coverings. The thought gave him a shiver. Sure, gruesome stuff was fascinating, but it also creeped him out.

"Okay, be brave," he told himself. He took a deep breath and lifted the corner of a tarp that was draped over a bed. "Ack," he squawked, staring into the empty eye sockets of a skeleton dressed in a bride's gown and veil. "Her new husband must have been really ugly—he scared her to death!" He gave a nervous laugh.

Nick moved on to the next shrouded shape. It looked like the traditional Halloween ghost with a sheet draped over it, a little taller than Nick. All it needed was eye holes and a scary mouth. He gulped and lifted the sheet. Bracing himself, he shined his light underneath. The figure had no head. A ragged line of red-tinged flesh showed above the shirt collar. "Ugh," he said. As the beam of his light moved downward, Nick gasped. The figure held its own ghastly head in the crook of its arm. Nick dropped the sheet and put his hand over his thumping heart. "That guy really lost his head," he said, in another weak attempt at a joke.

"Oh, man," Nick muttered, "I'm losing it —I'm talking to myself." He had a feeling being alone with these ghoulish monsters in the quiet building was even spookier than it would be on Fright Night. At least then there would be other people around—living and breathing *real* people. Where were all the tourists anyway?

He came to the gallows. He felt a moment of pride to see how good his repairs looked. You couldn't even tell the whole thing had been wrecked the night before. He scanned his light over the hanged man. The head hung at an angle inside the thick noose. At least there's no blood or gore with a hanging, Nick thought. A flash of color caught his attention and he focused the light on it. His heart sped up as he realized they were words. On the body of the dummy in blood-red letters someone had written a warning:

YOUR NEXT!

## Chapter 10.  Trouble in Two-Step Alley

"Your next?" Nick read out loud. "That wasn't there before, was it?" Surely he would have noticed when he hung up the dummy on the repaired scaffold.

He backed away from the gallows. He jogged over to the window and, with shaking fingers, grasped the walkie-talkie and pressed the 'talk' button. "Mandy, come in," he said. *Please*, he added silently. "Are you there? Mandy?"

"Yes, I hear you loud and clear," her voice replied. "What's up?"

"Any chance you can come to the Officers' Quarters? There's something I want you to see."

"Not more damage, I hope," she said.

"No, not exactly. Can you come over?"

"Sure. I think this area's pretty safe right now. With all the visitors around, no one would dare to try something. We'll be there in a few minutes. Over and out."

He decided to wait for them at the bottom of the stairs that led to the nearest casemate. He really didn't want to be in that room any longer. Between the creepy things under the sheets and the message on the dummy, he'd had enough.

He heard Peyton chattering about zombies before the girls came into sight. When he spotted them coming up the stairs from the parade grounds, he felt a great sense of relief. At least now he wasn't alone.

"So what did you find, Nick?" Mandy asked.

"I'll show you," he said. "Come on."

He led them to the dummy hanging on the gallows and pointed his flashlight at the writing. "So was that there before? I don't think so."

"Your next," read Mandy. "Whoever wrote it can't spell very well. It should be 'you're,' the contraction for 'you are'."

Nick rolled his eyes. Leave it to Mandy to turn it into an English lesson. "You missed the point," he said. "I don't remember seeing that when I hung up the dummy earlier today. That means someone wrote it between then and the time I came back from seeing you at the storerooms."

"No, it wasn't there this morning." Mandy pulled out her penlight to study the writing more closely. "Look," she said, "there's something else there."

"It's that eye picture," Peyton said. "The same one I saw under the bridge."

"And the same one on that necklace I found on the floor," Mandy said.

"Great," Nick said, "that means the intruder *did* drop the medallion." He gulped. "And it means this message is from him. He must have doubled back in Two-Step Alley and came out this way instead of where you were."

"What does it mean?" Peyton asked. "You're next for what?"

Nick shivered. "It's a threat. It's written on a dead guy. He's going to get me next."

"Don't be silly, Nick," said Mandy. "He's not going to hurt someone. That goes way beyond protesting Fright Night."

"Are you sure about that? Do we really know what his motives are? He knew I was patrolling here and he knew I would see this message." Nick shivered again. "I need to get out of here. Let's go eat lunch now."

Mandy sighed. "We can't. Brooke is going to take over for us at noon. Aunt Julie wants this area protected at all times. It's where most of the bad stuff is happening."

"No kidding," Nick retorted.

"We'll stay with you," Peyton offered. "Won't we, Mandy?"

"That's a good idea," agreed Mandy. "Right now there are so many people in the storerooms and casemates, I think it will be okay to leave those areas unguarded."

They could hear voices and heavy footfalls in the room below.

"Look at that guy!" a boy said. "He's gonna fall out of his chair!"

"An antique washboard," said a woman. "I bet clothes didn't last long getting scrubbed on one of those."

"They must be looking at the exhibit of old-fashioned stuff downstairs," Mandy said. "They'll make their way up here in a few minutes. Let's take a look in Two-Step Alley."

"Do we have to?" Nick demanded. "It's dark in there."

"We've each got a light," Peyton said. "With the three of us together, we'll be able to see."

"She's right," said Mandy. "Come on."

"Okay, okay," Nick muttered. At least Mandy wasn't afraid to lead the way. He was happy to let the girls go first. "I'll be the rearguard," he said.

Peyton glanced at him over her shoulder and said in a puzzled tone, "You're guarding my rear?"

Nick snorted and then grinned at her. "It's the way soldiers talk. It means I'm watching behind so no one can sneak up on us."

"Behind as in *bee*-hind?" Peyton said, giggling at her own joke.

"You're hilarious," Nick said.

With all three lights switched on, the children entered into Two-Step Alley.

"Why do we have to do this?" Nick said in a low voice. "The guy could be anywhere by now."

"Shh," Mandy warned. She tiptoed to the corner of the tunnel. "Lights off." She peeked around and then pulled her head back quickly. "There's someone down there," she whispered.

"Is it the bad guy or a g-ghost?" Peyton asked.

"I can't tell from here. Come on—slow and quiet." She edged around the corner.

As Peyton and Nick followed, Nick could make out a moving shape about half way down the alley. It reminded him of the figure he and Mandy had glimpsed in the Enlisted Men's Quarters. Human or spirit? A shiver rippled down his back. He couldn't tell either.

Nick saw an arm reach into the aperture in front of a rifle slot as if grabbing something and then the form seemed to melt into the blackness. Nick wiped sweat off his forehead, even though the tunnel was cool. What was going on? He could hear furtive sounds—rustling and scuffling. The toe of his sneaker caught on a brick sticking up a little higher than the rest in the floor and he stumbled. Trying to catch himself, he thrust out his hands. His flashlight launched through the air, landing somewhere in front of him with a rattle, and went out. Nick moaned.

The figure appeared again, stood still for a minute and then turned and fled.

"Turn your lights on!" Mandy said and took off after him.

Holding onto the wall with one hand and aiming her light at the ground with the other, Peyton followed. "Get him, Mandy!" she shouted.

"Wait!" said Nick. "I lost my flashlight!"

No one stopped.

"Darn it," Nick said, hobbling after them. He hurried as fast as he could on his throbbing foot, a hand against the wall so he wouldn't trip again. "Ouch!" he said, as he stepped on something lumpy and kind of squishy. It couldn't be a brick. He felt around on the ground. His fingers closed around an object and he lifted it toward the nearest rifle slot so he could see it. At first he couldn't tell what it was and then it dawned on him. "A rubber rat," he murmured. Its head had been cut off with a knife. "Gross!" he exclaimed.

Nick dropped the rat and ran after Mandy and Peyton.

## Chapter 11. The Witch's Curse

When Nick caught up with the girls, they stood outside Two-Step Alley, looking around at all the visitors.

"Rats, we lost him again," Mandy said.

"You mean 'rat'," said Nick, when he could catch his breath. "Come see what I found." He started back into the tunnel and then stopped. "Uh, I lost my light. You go ahead, Mandy."

His cousin sighed and turned on her penlight.

Was that "big chicken" Nick heard her mutter under her breath? Why did she always call him that? He wasn't afraid, just. . . *careful*.

"Where is it?" Mandy asked.

"A little farther along the tunnel—on the ground," Nick said, "right where the intruder was standing when we saw him."

Peyton waved her light back and forth on the brick floor. "What are we looking for?"

"A rat that lost its head," Nick said, "literally."

"Here it is," Mandy said. "Looks like a lump of black plastic." She picked it up.

"Ick," said Peyton. "Here's its head." She handed the piece to Mandy.

"Why would someone do that?" Mandy asked.

"It's another warning," said Nick. "Look, there's that Egyptian symbol again." He pointed at the body of the rat where the small eye design gleamed in the beam of Peyton's light.

"We'll show this to Aunt Julie," Mandy said. "Whoever this guy is, he's leaving his mark on everything he destroys. Come on—it must be almost noon. We need to meet Brooke." She headed up Two-Step Alley.

When the children arrived back in the Officers' Quarters, they found Brooke surveying the scaffold.

"You did a nice job fixing this up, Nick. It looks good as new."

Nick felt a moment of pride.

"But what's this?" Brooke pointed at the eye design drawn on the dummy and the misspelled message: YOUR NEXT!

"We think the intruder did that," said Mandy, "and this." She showed Brooke the rubber rat pieces. "Plus, I found a key necklace here on the floor this morning that has the same symbol." She pulled it out of her pocket.

Peyton tugged on her mother's shirt sleeve. "Remember we saw a picture like that under the bridge on the waterfront walk? Someone spray-painted it there and you said it's gra-feet-tee."

Brooke smiled. "Graffiti. Yes I do remember. I believe it's some kind of witchcraft symbol. There's a group in town that's into that stuff. They claim to draw some kind of energy from the Jonathan Buck monument because of the leg outline that appeared on the gravestone and couldn't be removed." She looked at Nick. "Has Mandy told you the legend about Colonel Buck and the witch's curse?"

Nick nodded. "When we walked by the cemetery last night on the way to the ice cream place, an acorn dropped from a tree and hit me on the head. Mandy said it might be the witch who did it, that her ghost still haunts Bucksport. Supposedly, back in the 1700s Buck ordered the woman to be hanged as a witch, but before she died, she put a curse on him."

"It's a bunch of nonsense, of course," Brooke said. "No witches were ever executed in Maine. Jonathan Buck wasn't even born until 25 years after the Salem witch trials in Massachusetts. He was a well-respected man and the founder of Bucksport, originally called Buckstown. As a Patriot, he fought against the British, who in retaliation, burned down his house, sawmill and everything else he owned."

"Why didn't the soldiers at Fort Knox fight off the British when they attacked Bucksport?" Mandy asked.

"This all happened before the fort was built. Construction didn't even begin until 1844. In Colonel Buck's time, the settlers were pretty much at the mercy of the British. Later, he did rebuild his home and his descendants still live in Bucksport today."

"So if the curse isn't true, why is the leg on the gravestone?" Nick asked, puzzled.

"Good question," said Brooke. "Buck's grandchildren put up the stone 75 years after his death. At first it looked fine. Then gradually the image of the leg appeared. They tried to get rid of it, but it kept coming back. It's a flaw in the granite, a stain that probably goes all the way through. Anyway, some bored newspaper reporter wrote a story about the leg, making up his own explanation of what caused it, and the

Witch's Curse was born. It became an urban legend."

"Too bad it's not true," Nick said, disappointed. "It's a good story."

"But it's not fair to Colonel Buck," said Peyton, frowning. "People should remember him for the good things he did, not something bad he didn't even do."

"You're right about that," Mandy said. "So Brooke, do you think a modern-day witch is wrecking things in the fort? We thought the intruder was a man, but maybe not."

"There are male witches, you know," said Nick. "They're called warlocks."

Brooke looked thoughtful. "I don't know why a witch would have a problem with Fright Night. You'd think it would be right up her—or his—alley. But it's something to think about. We need to know more about that eye design." She took out her phone, went to Google Search and asked: "What is the meaning of the witchcraft eye symbol?"

A page of data appeared on the screen and Brooke scanned down through it, reading phrases in a murmur. "The All-Seeing Eye of the ancient Egyptian goddess Maat could see into a person's soul. Eventually, this was viewed as something dangerous, not just examining, but intending harm and became known as the Evil Eye."

"Oh, great," Nick said, staring at the warning on the dummy's body, "the Evil Eye."

"What's the Evil Eye?" Peyton asked.

Nick tore his gaze away from the dummy and looked at Mandy. He didn't want to scare Peyton. What should he say?

Mandy just shrugged.

Nick gulped. He would have to tell it like it is. "The Evil Eye means um, it means. . . we've been cursed by a witch."

## Chapter 12.  A Discovery

"I'll keep these here in the office," Aunt Julie said, after Mandy handed her the rubber rat and the medallion with the strange design and described their eventful morning. "Things just get stranger and stranger," she added. "I'll be so glad when Fright Night is over." She sighed and set the rat pieces and necklace on a shelf. "Thanks for the patrolling you did. Why don't you take your lunch outside and enjoy the beautiful day? A volunteer I trust is taking over for Brooke in about an hour."

Nick breathed in the warm summer air. What a relief to be out of the chilly, dark parts of the fort. "Let's find a place to eat and then look at the grounds," he suggested. "I really want to get an idea of the layout. . . *and* see the big cannon."

At a bench perched on the hillside overlooking the mighty Penobscot River, they ate their Italian sandwiches and enjoyed the view. Down below to the right, a stone wall bordered Battery A, forming an angle where the huge cannon crouched like a black beast. Beyond that the Penobscot Narrows Bridge soared in all its majesty.

"That tower has the observation deck at the top," Mandy said, pointing at the obelisk on the right. "An elevator takes you up."

"It reminds me of the Washington Monument in D.C.," commented Nick, between bites. "They're probably about the same height."

"Not quite," said Mandy. "Aunt Julie says the towers are modeled after the Washington Monument but are about 100 feet shorter."

"They're still pretty tall," Nick replied. "I can't wait to go to the top."

Peyton slid a little closer to Nick. "You can see a long way up there. It's like being a bird in the sky."

"Hopefully, you won't be like a Maine seagull," Nick replied, remembering the time Mandy's family had taken him to Schoodic Point for a picnic and the embarrassing result.

"Why, what do they do?" the little girl asked.

"Well, they've been known to, um. . . doo-doo on people below."

Peyton giggled. "Euuw."

"Nick!" Mandy protested. "We're eating!"

Nick grinned at Peyton, his little buddy who appreciated his sense of humor, and then changed the subject. "Anyway, I can't wait to see that big baby up close." He gestured at the cannon with his last piece of sandwich. "I picked up a brochure at the Visitors' Center. It says here 'the large Rodman cannon in Battery A was extremely powerful, but slow to maneuver. Twelve men were needed to load the cannon. They used a mechanical hoist to lift the 450 pound cannonball.' Awesome. Are you girls almost done?" He crumpled up the sandwich wrap, tossed it at Mandy and grabbed a cookie. "Come on, let's get going."

Without even checking to see if the girls followed, Nick slipped and slid down the steep hill to Battery A, munching the cookie as he went, and strode across the grass to the huge cannon. He patted the warm metal of the cannon's carriage with affection and then climbed up onto the wall to take a peek down the tube. The opening was about a foot and a half across, wide enough for him to stick his whole head inside. Of course that blocked the light, so he withdrew his head and reached for his flashlight.

"Darn," he muttered, as he remembered breaking the light in the tunnel when he tripped. He would have to borrow one. "Hurry up!" he called to the girls, who had just reached the bottom of the hill. While he waited for them, he read more from the Fort Knox brochure he had been carrying around in his pocket. 'The tube weight is 50,000 pounds and the weight of the gunpowder charge was 100 pounds for a solid cannonball. At a 20 degree elevation, the cannon could fire a solid cannonball 5,579 yards'. Hmm, Nick thought. He knew a football field is 120 yards. He did some quick mental math. That was the distance of about 46 football fields. Huh? Was the cannon supersonic or something? Looking at it another way, with 1760 yards in a mile, that came out to. . . over three miles! Wow!

He studied a nearby information panel that showed an actual photo from the 1800s of four men in old-fashioned clothes priming the cannon to fire. He sighted down the barrel of the gun. A bunch of trees were in the way. What use was a cannon that could fire three miles if you couldn't see that far? Of course in those days, all the trees had probably been cleared to give as far a view as possible. Plus, it would make the weapon really powerful. A cannonball fired at a ship a half mile away would hit with tremendous force.

Ba-boom! It would blow that bath toy right outta the water!

"About time you got here," Nick said, as the girls approached. "Can I borrow your light for a minute, Peyton?"

"What do you need it for?" she asked, handing him the penlight. "It's sunny out here."

"Come here and I'll show you," he said, giving her a hand up onto the wall. He aimed the light inside the cannon. Some small stones and a plastic water bottle lay in the tube.

Peyton stuck her head next to his and peered down the barrel. "No gold," she said, disappointed.

"No, they keep all the gold at the *other* Fort Knox," Nick said, "the one in Kentucky."

"Too bad," she replied. "It would be fun to find a real treasure."

"You're right about that. Mandy and I have found a few treasures in the past, haven't we, Mandy?"

No reply.

Nick looked around but his cousin had disappeared. "Where's Mandy?"

Peyton glanced around too. "Oh, there she is—by the thing that looks like an oven."

"Let's take a look," Nick said, handing the light back to Peyton. He headed for a brick structure about the size of a Humvee with a wide chimney on top. On the way, he looked at the map of the fort. "It's the hot-shot furnace."

Why is it called that?" she asked. "Does it like to show off a lot?"

Nick laughed. "I don't think so. It says here this is where they heated up the cannonballs so when they hit a ship, they would set it on fire. Cool, huh?"

"Cool but warm at the same time," the little girl said, grinning at him.

"Hey, guys, over here," Mandy's voice said. They could hear her, but couldn't see her.

"Where are you?" Nick asked.

"Look in the window," said Mandy.

Nick and Peyton ducked down to peer up into the arched opening of the furnace. They could see Mandy's head silhouetted against the sky at the other end where the cannonballs would have been loaded. Nick shined Peyton's light inside. It revealed three rusty metal rails that formed two grooves to hold the balls. They would have rolled from Mandy's end down the sloping rails to be heated above a coal fire and then unloaded from Nick's end.

"There's a lot of junk in here," he said. Loose debris—pieces of stone, brick and metal—partially filled the grooves.

"Can I see?" Peyton asked.

Nick moved over so she could squeeze in beside him. She stuck her hand into the furnace.

"Ouch, ouch, it's really hot in here!" the girl said.

"What?" Alarmed, Nick stepped back.

"Just kidding!" Peyton said. "I was pretending my hand was a cannonball being heated up."

Nick shook his head. Sometimes she got a little carried away.

"Can you boost me up for a minute? I thought I saw something."

Mandy had walked around to their side of the furnace. "What is it?" she asked.

"I'm not sure," said Peyton.

They joined together to boost her up and all three peered into the furnace. Peyton clicked on her light. "Right there," she said. A piece of dark metal stuck up above the rocks and bricks. The little girl moved a few chunks away and pulled on the metal. It came away suddenly from the debris.

"Who-o-oa," said Nick, losing his balance at the sudden lurch.

The children fell in a heap on the ground with Peyton on top.

"Look," she said. "I found some keys!"

## Chapter 13. The Caretaker's Keys

The children stared at Peyton's find.

"Keys," said Mandy in astonishment. "They look really old." She took them from Peyton and spread them out on her palm.

Six dark brown keys, rough and a little rusty with open oval tops, were attached to a metal ring about three inches across.

"Wowser!" said Nick. Can I see them?"

Mandy handed him the ring of keys.

"They're heavy," he said, hefting them. "They must be made of iron." He spread them out as Mandy had. "Each one has different teeth so they must go to different locks."

"What do you think they open?" Peyton asked, her eyes shining with excitement. "Six treasure chests?"

Nick snorted. "Yup, you and my sister Christianne will get along great. That's what she always thinks too—if you find a key, it must lead to treasure."

"Well, in a way she's right," said Mandy, thinking back to their past adventures. "It depends on your meaning of treasure. We did find those gold coins in the old prospector's cabin in California and the silver dollars in the ghost town in Nevada. Even when it wasn't money, like the letters and diaries, it sometimes meant we got a reward."

"True," Nick agreed, "and whatever we opened with the key helped us solve the mystery."

"So it could be treasure!" replied Peyton. She held out her hand. "Can I have them back?"

After Nick passed them to her, Peyton singled out the largest key, about six inches long with a double tooth. "I bet this one opens the front door."

"The front door of what?" Mandy asked.

"The fort, of course," said Peyton.

Mandy stared at the key. "The main gate," she said. "Wow, you could be right."

"That can't be it. Julie used a small key to unlock a padlock on the gate," Nick reminded them.

"But, Nick, that's probably pretty new. Back in the old days, they would have used a big key to lock the gate—just like this." She touched the key in Peyton's hand.

"Cool," said Nick. "What else in the fort would need to be locked up?" He studied the other keys. "Maybe the gunpowder?"

"I bet that's it. The fort has lots of powder magazines and the four smaller keys could be for those. That just leaves one."

Peyton held up the other large key, which had a single tooth that bent in two places.

"Hmm," Mandy murmured, "Officer's Quarters, storage rooms, bakery, Enlisted Men's Quarters—I doubt if they would need to lock any of those areas."

"What about those little white buildings with the stairways going down to Battery A and Battery B?" Peyton asked. "Mom calls them the Doghouses. They wouldn't want the bad guys sneaking *up* the stairs."

Nick nodded. "That makes sense."

"But there are two buildings and only one key," Mandy pointed out.

"The key could fit both locks," reasoned Nick.

They all thought about that for a moment.

"I don't think so," Mandy finally said. "The buildings are too far apart. They would need a key for each one so they could be locked or unlocked fast in a battle."

"Yeah, I suppose so," Nick agreed. "So this is a mystery key."

"Yay! A mystery for us to solve!" said Peyton, holding up the keys in triumph. "I can be a detective just like you."

Nick peeked into the hot shot furnace. "So why do you think the keys were in there?"

"I've been thinking about that," Mandy said. "I can come up with only three reasons— either someone lost them, threw them away or hid them."

"How could someone lose them in a furnace?" Nick asked. "The person would have to be *in* there. Anyway, the keys are too big to be carried in a pocket. The ring was probably attached to a man's belt, like you see in old movies."

"No one would throw away the keys to the fort. . . would they?" Peyton said, frowning. "They might need them again sometime."

"No, I don't think they would," said Mandy. "So how did they end up in the furnace? My best guess is someone hid them."

"Who would do that?" Nick asked.

"Hmm, I wonder what happened to the keys after Sergeant Hegyi died back in 1900. He must have carried them everywhere, probably attached to *his* belt."

"The Army would have taken the keys off his belt before they buried him," said Nick.

"Then what?" Mandy asked.

"Maybe there was a new caretaker?" Peyton suggested. "*Somebody* had to take care of the fort after Sergeant Hegyi!"

"I'm sure we can find out," said Mandy.

"I can't see *any* caretaker leaving the keys in the hot shot furnace, can you?" Nick asked.

"No, not really," said Mandy. "The keys were too important."

Peyton squinted in thought. "So why would someone *hide* the keys?"

"Good question," said Mandy. "Usually people hide things because they don't want other people to find them."

"This is a long shot," Nick said, "but maybe the intruder is using them to get into the fort. Maybe he found them somewhere and stashes them in the hot shot furnace so he can get in and out whenever he wants. The main gate has a padlock now, but there might be another door we don't know about that the keys open. Are there other ways into the fort?"

"Only one I know about," said Mandy. "Aunt Julie said for a long time visitors to the fort used to come in from the parking lot by walking over the ramparts and down some stairs, through the dry moat, to a door into the casemates and Two-Step Alley."

"Did you say Two-Step Alley?" Nick exclaimed, thinking about his recent encounter with the intruder there. "That's where the guy who cut off the rat's head was hanging out today. . . and it leads right into the Officers' Quarters where the warning was written on the dummy. I bet he *has* been using the keys. From Two-Step Alley he can get to just about anywhere in the fort in a few minutes. He messes things up, ducks into the passage, and escapes without anyone seeing him. We need to check out that door. . . right now!"

## Chapter 14.  Doghouse to Dungeon

"How do we get there?" Nick asked.

"I know, I know!" Peyton said, jangling the keys. She pointed up the hillside. "We're pretty close—just up and over the ramparts. Follow me!" The little girl marched up the steep incline with Mandy and Nick behind. At the top was the bench where they had eaten lunch. She led them over the ramparts and down a stone stairway to a grassy area between two walls.

"Oh, this is where I looked for the intruder this morning," Nick said, recognizing the brick walkway with an open door at either end.

"Yeah, this is the dry moat," Mandy explained. "Moats around castles usually had water in them, but not forts. The fort is five-sided and the dry moat goes around three of those sides, between these two walls. If the enemy got into this area, they could be shot at from both directions. She pointed to the rifle loopholes in the sides of the long stone walls. "The one on the right is actually Two-Step Alley and the one on the left is called Long Alley. One is higher than the other so soldiers firing guns from the slots wouldn't hit each other."

"Wow, a deadly crossfire!" Nick said in admiration. "Whoever planned Fort Knox sure knew what he was doing."

They stopped in front of the doorway leading into the interior of the fort. A big green wooden door with a curved top stood open, held in that position by a chain. A padlock held the chain to a bolt.

"Look at that bar!" exclaimed Peyton. "It could be pushed across to lock the door from the inside."

Mandy studied it up close. "But there's no key hole. Our keys don't go to this door."

"So the intruder isn't using them to get in this way," said Peyton, hands on hips. "They wouldn't work for him either."

"That's too bad," Nick said. "It would be easy for him to leave them in the furnace on his way in and out of the fort. . . *and* easy for us to stop him now that we have the keys."

"This door must be locked at night using the bolt," Mandy said. "It looks like the padlock is just to keep the door chained open in the day time. So Aunt Julie must have the key to that too. Rats."

"He's getting in somehow," Peyton said, stating the obvious.

"There must be a door we don't know about," said Nick.

Mandy's eyebrows scrunched together in thought. "If there is, I don't know where. I'm curious about the main gate. Even though they use a padlock for it now, I want to know if any of these keys fit the old lock. Come on." Mandy led them inside. She pointed at stone steps going up. "See, here's the entrance to the Officers' Quarters and beyond that, of course, is Two-Step Alley."

"Very handy for the intruder," said Nick.

They passed through several casemates, hopped down the steps to the parade grounds and followed the granite walkway to the main gate. Visitors wandered in and out of the entrance, stopping to view the skeleton in the canoe and the giant spider in the lobster trap. The children stopped outside the gate and waited.

"Shoot," Mandy murmured. "There are too many people around to try the keys. They would wonder what we're up to. We'll have to do it later."

Nick had been studying the gate. "Are these the original doors or something they put up later on?"

The two metal gates were made of vertical black bars crisscrossed with heavy-duty black mesh. A shiny silver chain and padlock hung from a loop on both the doors, one right beside the winged ghoul that had been added for Fright Night. Nick had seen Julie open the locks with a small key.

"Maybe not," Mandy replied. "They don't look strong enough to keep out determined enemies."

"Plus the bad guys could shoot right through these gates," said Peyton.

"Well, I don't see a keyhole anywhere except in the padlocks," Nick said. "Unless there's one under this sign screwed to the gate that says 'Property of the State of Maine: Breaking or entering these premises or the removal of any parts or contents thereof is a Class E Crime.' Hmm, I wonder what a Class E crime is."

"I don't know, but it sounds serious," Mandy replied. "Maybe the intruder didn't see that sign."

Nick shrugged. "I don't think he cares. If criminals worried about getting caught, they wouldn't commit crimes. Anyway, our keys don't open the gates."

"Phooey," said Peyton. "I really thought the big key would open the fort." The corners of her mouth drooped in disappointment.

"No worries," said Nick. "They're still cool keys. While we're right here, could we check out the Doghouse? I've wanted to take a look in there since the intruder escaped that way the other night." A drop of sweat trickled down his neck as he remembered how he had *not* wanted to go into that black hole at the time.

"Sure, why not?" said Mandy. "We've got the afternoon to explore."

They walked left along the front of the fort to the little white building with a sign that said Battery B. They could see across the river to Bucksport.

When Nick stepped from the bright sunshine into the murky interior, he shivered. Just as he suspected, stairs led down—*way* down—and disappeared into darkness.

"Lights on," said Peyton, clicking the button of her purple mini light.

"Hold onto the railing," Mandy advised, turning on her light and starting down the steps.

"You girls go ahead," Nick said in relief, "my light is broken."

Peyton glanced over her shoulder and grinned. "Are you guarding my rear again?"

Nick chuckled. "You got it."

The children worked their way down the stairway. At the bottom, the passageway forked. One way took them to an empty room with window openings that let in the daylight. Rusty metal semi circles on the floor showed it must have been a gun emplacement for probably some smaller cannons. The other direction took them to a dirt-floored space with bars.

"Watch this," said Peyton. She ducked into a skinny passageway to the right of the dirt-floored room. In a moment her light appeared behind the room, shining through an opening faced with black iron bars. She held the light under her chin and made a gruesome face. "Ooooooo," she moaned.

"Cool," said Nick. "What is this place—the dungeon?"

"Maybe," said Mandy. "It makes sense though that there needed to be a jail of some sort in case they took prisoners in a battle."

"Or maybe it was a place to keep gunpowder and ammo if there was a battle going on," Nick suggested. "The main powder magazines are too far away to do much good for the cannon that were here."

Peyton scampered the rest of the way around the passage and popped out on the left. She aimed her light at Nick's face. "Did I scare you?"

Nick raised a hand to shield his eyes. "I was shaking in my boots."

"You have boots on?" the little girl asked, moving her light to his feet. "No, you're wearing sneakers! Are you trying to trick me?"

Nick ruffled her hair. "It's just an expression. You looked *very* scary. You know, if this was a jail or even a powder magazine, they had to be able to lock it—with a key."

"You're right," Mandy said. Her light traced the opening of the room. "There's nothing here now to lock, but there must have been when the fort was active. One of our keys might have fit."

"This is kind of a bummer," said Nick. "We find these awesome keys and they don't go to anything."

"Don't give up, Nick," Peyton said. "We'll solve the mystery!"

They walked in the opposite direction, down some stairs and out into the sunshine.

Nick blinked, dazzled for a moment. Sensing someone behind him, he looked back at the dark doorway. He thought he saw a person standing back in the shadows—a tall man in uniform, with a bushy mustache, short white beard and a wide-brimmed cavalry hat. He blinked again.

The figure was gone.

## Chapter 15. The Soldier's Ghost

"Hey, I think someone is in there," Nick said, pointing back inside the gray stone structure. "He looked like an old-time soldier."

"Hmm, maybe a Civil War re-enactor?" said Mandy. "Aunt Julie didn't say anything about that happening today though. Sometimes the re-enactors pitch their tents and shoot rifles and stuff."

"Yeah, and it's *really* loud," Peyton added. "I have to cover my ears."

Nick walked a few steps back inside, but didn't see anyone. "Oh, well, I probably imagined it."

"Maybe it was Sergeant Hegyi's ghost," Peyton suggested, "looking for his keys. She held them up and they clanked together.

A shiver tiptoed up Nick's back. "Man, I hope not. He'll be after us." It was bad enough to worry about an intruder, but a ghost too? He glanced over his shoulder and then moved on, glad to be out in the bright sunlight.

The children arrived at Battery B. A Rodman cannon, like the Battery A gun but without a tall, sturdy carriage supporting it, sat forlornly with its muzzle resting on the edge of the granite wall.

"This is pretty sad," Nick commented, "compared to how it used to look. There's a picture in the museum of a long row of cannons that was here, ready for action with a pile of cannonballs behind each one."

"I wonder where all the cannons went?" said Mandy. "Anyway, let's go down and take a look at the wharf."

They walked down to the large grassy area edged with granite blocks that jutted into the river. Stone steps descended into the water.

"Awesome! A stairway to Atlantis," Nick said, referring to the lost city that sank beneath the sea. He peered down into the murky depths. "It looks a little slippery." Dark green seaweed covered the lower steps, floating in the water like the tentacles of a sea monster.

"Uncle Gabe brought us here once from Dyer Cove in his boat, *Sea Hag*," said Mandy. "It's really only safe to land at high tide because of the seaweed." She pointed at the ring attached to the granite edging. "We tied up there, climbed up the top three steps, and actually got in free. It was really fun to travel here by water."

"But Mandy, what about the sign?" Peyton asked. "People aren't supposed to land here." She indicated the large red-and-white sign on a tilted post that warned: *No Trespassing, Private Dock, No Landing.*

"This was a couple of years ago," Mandy said. "The sign wasn't there then."

"Aww, that's too bad you won't be able to come here by boat anymore."

Something clicked in Nick's mind. "By boat—that's it! That's how the intruder escaped the other night! When he went down the stairway to Battery B, he must have had a boat tied up here. I heard a motor, but thought it was just someone going home late from fishing."

"Hmm, so the dirt bike in the parking lot didn't belong to him," said Mandy.

"Unless there were two intruders and they didn't come together," Peyton reasoned.

Nick shook his head. "I hope not. It's hard enough to keep track of one bad guy, let alone two."

"Maybe Aunt Julie will hear from the police about the license plate today," Mandy said. "It would sure help if we knew who owns the dirt bike. Anyway, the guy in the boat must have been going over to Bucksport. Maybe he lives there."

"Or Verona Island," said Peyton, referring to the big island in the middle of the river. "Did you see which way the boat went, Nick?"

"I couldn't see it, just heard the motor. I don't know which direction it was going." Nick frowned, trying to remember details.

"This evening let's go down to the waterfront in Bucksport and check out the boats," Mandy suggested. "You never know—we might notice something."

"Good idea," said Nick, who was eyeing the impressive wall that rose up from the wharf in two tiers, all the way to the path outside the main gate. "I'd love to climb that wall. It looks like the side of a step pyramid."

"It would be fun," Peyton said, "but we can't." She pointed to another sign. *Please— DON'T CLIMB WALLS.*

Nick sighed. "Rats. I suppose they're trying to keep the fort as safe as possible. If a kid fell on that, he'd probably end up in the Emergency Room. So how do we get back up to the Visitors' Center?" He frowned. "Do we have to go back up the stairs to the Doghouse?" He really didn't feel up to meeting the old Sergeant's ghost—if it was a ghost—in those dark passages. Would he try to get the keys away from them?

"There's another way," Peyton offered. "We just go back to Battery B and follow the path that zigzags up to the top." She gestured in the general direction. "It comes out right near the Visitors' Center."

"Sounds good to me," said Nick. He wouldn't admit it to the girls, of course, but he was relieved to stay outside. "Lead the way."

Still holding the ring of keys, Peyton marched up the hillside to where the lone cannon guarded Battery B, with Nick and Mandy behind her. They followed a well-worn grassy road that wound its way back up to the main path in front of the fort.

Back at the Visitors' Center, Nick said, "I feel like I have a better idea of the layout of the fort now. Are there any areas we didn't see?"

Mandy thought for a minute. "Well, we didn't go into Long Alley yet. I think you peeked in there this morning, Nick. It's like Two-Step Alley without the two-steps and it's longer because it goes around the outside edge of the fort. Aunt Julie said people have seen strange things there. Do you want to go take a look?"

Nick gulped. He didn't want to know what the 'strange things' were. "Uh, no, that's okay.

One tunnel is pretty much the same as another."
*Yeah, dark and spooky*, he thought.

"So what do you want to do while we're waiting for Aunt Julie to take us back to her house?" Mandy asked.

Peyton had gotten her iPad from the staff room and sat at a table, playing Minecraft, building walls and zapping zombies.

Hunger pains gnawed at Nick's stomach. "Are there any more cookies?"

"I'll go see," Mandy offered, heading to the back room.

Nick meandered around, studying the displays. In a glass case an old rifle and a Cavalry sword were displayed. Boy, he wished he could touch them. How awesome it would be to actually hold a weapon that had seen action over a hundred years ago!

He loved the old photos showing the rows of cannon in place—the way a fort *should* look. In another photo men stood by a crane-like structure called a derrick lifting a huge stone block from the waterfront. What hard work it must have been to get all that heavy granite to the site and put it together like a giant jigsaw puzzle to make such an amazing fort.

He moved to another picture. It showed a man with a short white beard, bushy mustache and piercing eyes dressed in a uniform and Cavalry style hat. Nick's breath caught in his throat. The guy in the photo looked *exactly* like the man he saw in the tunnel near Battery B.

He read the caption under the picture: *Ordnance Sergeant Leopold Hegyi, U.S. Army, 1832-1900. Fortkeeper at Fort Knox for 13 long and lonely years. . .*

## Chapter 16.  A Close Encounter

"You really saw Sergeant Hegyi's ghost?" Peyton asked, her brown eye's wide.

The children lounged in the livingroom of Aunt Julie's house after dinner that evening.

Nick shrugged. He really didn't want it to be true. "Maybe it was his look-alike or his great-grandson or someone dressed up in a costume who wanted to look like him. All I know is the man I saw as we left the tunnel at Battery B looked exactly like the picture of Sergeant Hegyi in the museum."

"I think it *is* his ghost," said Mandy. "There's too much weird stuff happening for it not to be. I think he's upset and trying to tell us something."

"Huh?" Nick said, startled. "What are you saying? A ghost is trying to talk to us?"

"Well, he's trying to communicate, but not in actual words." Mandy wrinkled her freckled nose as she thought. "You know how they say a ghost might haunt a place because he or she has unfinished business? I get the feeling that's what's happening with Sergeant Hegyi. He dedicated thirteen years of his life to taking care of the fort and died suddenly. Maybe he left something undone and he wants us to help him."

Peyton jingled the keys. "What could it be?"

Nick stared at the keys, mesmerized. A thought dropped into his mind. "Uh, maybe the Sergeant isn't trying to *get* the keys. Maybe he wanted us to find them." He couldn't believe he said that.

"If that's so," said Mandy, "then at least one of those keys must unlock something important. It wouldn't have to be a door."

"Maybe he'll give us another clue," Peyton said. "Until then we'll keep his keys safe." She looked around the room and her eyes lit on a buck's head mounted on the wall above the fireplace. "Let's hang them on the deer. Nick, can you reach up there?"

Nick took the keys and stretched up to loop the key ring over one of the antler points. The twelve-point buck gazed at him with glassy brown eyes. Nick patted him on the nose. "Nice deer," he said with a nervous laugh.

"So let's head to the waterfront to check out the boats," Mandy suggested. "Maybe we'll get lucky. I already asked Aunt Julie if we could go for a walk."

Nick's face brightened. "Can we stop on the way for more ice cream? I want to try Campfire S'mores." He dug in his pocket and pulled out a crumpled handful of dollar bills. "I'll treat you both."

The girls grinned at each other. "Hey, thanks! Let's go."

As they walked on the sidewalk past the Buck monument, Nick glanced at the outline of the leg with an uneasy feeling. Even though he knew the legend of the witch was made-up, the stain on the stone still creeped him out. It really did look like a leg. What were the chances of that happening for no reason? He shivered and hurried after the girls.

With cones in hand, they crossed Main St. and walked down a short side street to the town wharf. Ten boats of various sizes were moored there. Licking their ice cream, they strolled along the dock, studying each one.

"Here's *Lil' Toot*," said Peyton with affection. "It's like the boat in the book Little Toot except it's a tour boat instead of a tug boat. It's fun to ride on."

Painted red and white, the boat boasted a festive candy-cane striped awning and an American flag on the bow. Taking up a long stretch of dock was a big three-story steamboat with *American Glory* written on the transom. Tourists walked down the gangplank to the wharf and wandered along the waterfront.

"That boat comes up from Belfast," Peyton explained. "Mom said from here it goes to Bar Harbor."

Most of the other vessels were boats with outboard motors and no names. The smallest one, black on the outside and gray on the inside, bobbed beside the wharf. As Nick strolled past it, a red image on the stern caught his eye. He stopped and peered at it.

"Hey, guys," he said in a low voice. "Check this out."

The girls leaned over to get a better look.

"The eye symbol," Mandy murmured. "This boat must belong to the intruder."

They glanced around to make sure no one had noticed them.

"We should write down the registration number," said Nick. He rummaged in his pockets, but as usual, he had nothing to write with.

"I'll do it," said Peyton, slipping out her cute puppy notebook and pencil. "ME 2216 AW," she recited. "If we give this to Gram, she might be able to find out who owns it and then we'll know who's been getting into the fort!"

"Hey, what are you kids doing?" a gruff voice demanded.

They whirled around to face a tall, skinny man with long, greasy black hair and stubble on his chin. His jeans and plaid shirt were dirty and torn. He had an ugly scowl and teeth stained brown.

Nick swallowed. The stranger pretty much looked the way he imagined the intruder would look. He was *so* glad he hadn't come face-to-face with him in Two-Step Alley or the Battery B doghouse. He was scarier than any ghost. Nick crossed his arms and took a step backward.

"Uh, we were wondering about this design on the boat," said Mandy in a brave voice. "Do you know what it means?"

The man spit into the water. "That's Drake Duggen's boat. He's into that witchcraft stuff. You better watch out or he might put on a spell on you." He said the last sentence while leering at them with a nasty grin. He sauntered on to the next boat, untied the line that held it to the dock, and jumped in. In a few moments he had the motor started and trolled out into the river, headed in the direction of Verona Island.

Nick took a deep breath and tried to slow his galloping heart. "Wow, that guy sure looked like he could have been the intruder, but the boat with the 'evil eye' isn't his."

"But we know the intruder's name!" Peyton exclaimed. "I wrote it down—Drake Duggen. I'll find out if Mom knows him."

"Oh, I forgot to tell you that Aunt Julie heard from the police about the dirt bike parked at the fort," said Mandy. "It turns out it belongs to a teenage boy who got a ride with some friends to Bangor and he left the bike there overnight."

"So it looks like the intruder is working alone," Nick said. "That's good."

Mandy shook her head. "We still don't know that for sure. He might have had someone with him in the boat." She thought for a moment. "We need to find out about the witchcraft going on in town."

"Are there really witches nowadays?" Nick asked. "I thought that was long ago stuff or just in fairy tales."

"There are people who *call* themselves witches," Mandy replied. "I don't know if they can really do magic or not. Who in town would know about it?"

"I know who," said Peyton. "There's an old lady who lives behind the cemetery. Some people call her a witch, but Mom says she just wants to be left alone with her cats for company. On Halloween, kids dare each other to knock on her door, but she keeps the light off and the shades pulled down. Some people say she knows everything that goes on in town."

"Do you think she would talk to us?" Mandy asked.

"She might," Peyton said. "Maybe we could bring her something. Gram makes her peanut brittle once in awhile and takes it over."

"I saw some on a plate in the fridge," said Mandy. "If we head back now and ask for a few pieces, we could visit her before it gets too late."

"Great," muttered Nick, "just great. First a ghost, then a guy as ugly as an ogre and now a witch. Never a dull moment in Bucksport, Maine."

They hurried back to the house. The setting sun threw long shadows across their path.

Aunt Julie wrapped some peanut brittle in tinfoil and handed it to Mandy. "It's nice of you to take this over to Sadie. I think she gets kind of lonely. Tell her I said 'hello' and make sure you're home before dark."

"We will. Thanks, Aunt Julie," Mandy said, tucking the packet of candy in her jacket pocket.

As they walked past the monument of Colonel Buck again, Nick shivered. The light-colored granite of the stone almost seemed to glow in the gathering dusk, making the dark outline of the leg stand out clearer than ever. So what if people said it wasn't true? It *could* have come from a curse.

And now here he was on his way to visit a possible witch.

## Chapter 17.  A Visit to the Witch

"This is Sadie's house," Peyton said. She marched up to the front door and knocked.

Nick thought the house would look scary on Halloween night, or any night for that matter. Paint peeled off the dull gray siding and the porch creaked as they stepped onto its rotting boards. Some kind of vine with leaves the size of dinner plates twined around the posts and hung over the windows and door. Nick wondered if the witch had to hack through them to get out or if she just muttered a curse that made them shrink back. He shuffled his feet and wiped his sweating hands on his jeans as they waited.

"Aww, too bad, nobody's home," he said, turning to leave. "We'll have to try another time."

Just then the door squealed open.

"What do you want?" said a voice as rusty as the door hinges. The old woman didn't look like a witch—no black robe, no pointy hat, no wart on her nose. She wore gray sweatpants, a Red Sox sweatshirt and pink sneakers. Her gray hair was pinned back in a neat bun.

Nick felt kind of disappointed that she looked like someone's grandmother.

"Hi, Sadie, it's me, Peyton," said the little girl. "This is my cousin Mandy and her cousin Nick. Gram says 'hi' and sent some peanut brittle."

Mandy took the package out of her pocket and handed it to Sadie. "Um, we wondered if we could talk to you for a few minutes. We're trying to solve the mystery of who is damaging things at the fort and why. You might be able to help."

The woman frowned. "I've been hearing about strange goings-on at the fort. I blame it on that Fright Night rubbish—turning a historical site into a circus sideshow. It's a real shame." Her voice lost its rusty sound after a few sentences. "Here, come into the parlor and sit. I can't be standing on these old pins for long."

She shuffled into the nearest room and snapped on a floor lamp. It illuminated a shabby brown couch and two faded blue chairs. A spring had punched through the back of one chair and some of its stuffing spilled out. Sadie eased herself down into the other chair and the children sat in a row on the sofa.

"I kind of agree with you," Mandy said, "but Fright Night helps raise a lot of money used to repair the fort, so I can't really be against it. Aunt Julie says there's never enough money to do all that needs to be done."

"No doubt that's true," replied Sadie. "My own house is going to 'wrack and ruin' for the same reason. So how can I help you?"

Mandy took a deep breath. "Well, there's an intruder who is somehow getting into the fort and wrecking props for Fright Night. He seems to be leaving a red eye symbol behind as his sign."

"We saw the same eye on a boat at the dock," added Peyton. "A guy told us it belonged to a man named Drake Duggen. Do you know him?"

Sadie snorted with contempt. "The Duggens—a family that gives our town a bad name. All of them—mother, father and three grown children—practice witchcraft at its worst and are proud of it."

Nick wasn't sure if he really wanted to know, but he asked, "Uh, what kind of things do they do?"

"Spells, curses, rituals at midnight, and that sort of nonsense." Sadie shook her head in disgust. "One night I heard noises in the cemetery. When I looked out the upstairs window, I saw figures dressed in black, chanting under a full moon. Of course, I called the police straight away, but by the time they arrived, the Duggens had dissolved into the darkness, as they're so good at doing."

"But why would they be destroying stuff at the fort?" Mandy asked. "You'd think they would be happy about Fright Night."

"Yeah, it's right up their alley," Nick agreed. He jumped as something brushed against his leg. A black cat arched its back and hissed at him. Nick leaned back and raised his hands to ward off the fierce creature. "Uh, n-nice kitty," he stuttered.

"Don't pay any attention to Shadow," Sadie said. "She's not used to company." She shooed the cat away from Nick.

A big, fluffy gray cat with glowing yellow eyes rubbed against Peyton's legs. She reached down and gave it a pat. "Hi, Mellow, how's it going?"

Sadie's black eyes squinted as she thought about Mandy's question. "It could be the Duggens are just trying to cause trouble, which they love to do, or maybe they feel Fright Night makes a mockery of the black arts and they want to stop it. I don't really know. All I can say is do be careful. They are not people you want to stir up. They can make your life miserable."

Nick hesitated before asking the next question, feeling a little foolish. "Um, could they use magic to get in and out of the fort?"

The old woman considered his words before answering. "Not with a spell or anything like that. I have heard though there's a secret passage built for the soldiers to escape through in case the fort was overrun by the enemy."

Mandy and Nick stared at each other and then back at Sadie. "Do you know where it is?" Mandy asked.

"When my older brother was a young boy, before I was born, our mother took him to Fort Knox. He said he remembers an opening in the wall in one corner of the parade grounds that supposedly led all the way down to the waterfront."

"Wow!" exclaimed Peyton. "That would explain how the intruder could get in and out when the doors are locked. He would come out right down by the water stairs where he tied his boat."

Mandy frowned. "I don't remember an opening like that on the parade grounds. Do you?"

"No, but we weren't really looking for one," said Nick. "We can check it out tomorrow. It would sure explain a lot. . . the intruder would have an easy way into the Officers' Quarters and Two-Step Alley."

Mandy noticed it looked gloomy outside the parlor window. "We better get going. Aunt Julie said to be home before dark." She jumped up. "Thanks, Sadie. The things you told us should help a lot."

"Yeah, thanks. Nice to meet you." Nick added, warily sidestepping the cats on the way out.

Peyton waved goodbye to Sadie. "Enjoy the peanut brittle."

Outside, the sky wasn't as dark as it seemed from inside Sadie's house.

"Good, we can still make it in time," Mandy said. She snapped on her flashlight.

Peyton did the same. "Let's take the shortcut," she said. "Come on, I'll show you." She waded through the long grass in Sadie's yard, pushed through an overgrown hedge and followed the chain link fence along the back of the cemetery. Part of the fence had been pulled down. "Do you think the Duggens did this?"

"It wouldn't surprise me," Nick murmured. "They wouldn't let a mere fence stop them from dastardly deeds in the cemetery at midnight." He shivered. He sure didn't want to see them out the window. His room faced the graveyard, but he kept the shade pulled down at night.

"This is so exciting," said Mandy, "a secret passage. If we can block it somehow, the intruder won't be able to get into the fort. We've got to find it!"

As they stepped into Aunt Julie's backyard, Nick gasped. The beam of Peyton's light revealed a flash of red paint on the trunk of a big oak tree. "Look at that!" he said in a hoarse voice, pointing at the tree. "The Evil Eye. He knows where we are!"

Below the threatening symbol, two words jumped out at them.

**GO HOME!**

## Chapter 18. The Secret Tunnel

Nick was still nervous the next morning when they piled into Julie's car and headed for the fort. The intruder knew who they were. He knew where they were staying. He knew they were hunting him. If it was Drake Duggen, which would seem to be the case from the trail of red eye symbols, they were in big trouble. The guy might cast a spell on them and turn them all into toads. . .or do something much worse. Nick sure wasn't looking forward to guard duty at the fort today.

He opened his mouth to ask Julie a question. Mandy caught his eye and shook her head. The night before, they had argued and he had reluctantly agreed not to say anything about the Duggens.

"I don't want to worry Aunt Julie even more," Mandy had said. "We don't have any proof the Duggens are causing the trouble at the fort. We'll be extra careful and watch everyone like hawks. There's just one more day to get through and then it will be Fright Night."

"You children are quiet this morning," said Aunt Julie, as they drove toward the Penobscot Narrows Bridge. "Did you get enough sleep?"

"Sure," Mandy replied, giving Nick another warning look. "We're just thinking about today. It's hard to believe Fright at the Fort is tonight."

Nick thought it best not to say anything. He craned his neck to peer at the first of the two bridge towers that soared up like a skyscraper. Thick cables stretching from the tower to the bridge made a cool pattern against the sky. Turning his head to the right and looking across the water, he could see the fort hunkered against the hillside like a crouching dragon full of dark secrets.

Julie sighed. "I'm so glad. If we can just make it through the day, everything should be okay. I keep reminding myself that whatever happens, the fort will survive. I just don't want anyone getting hurt."

*I'll second that*, Nick thought.

"There will be a lot of volunteers putting the final touches to the sets today," she continued, "and visitors, too, who find it interesting to see behind the scenes before the event. We'll clear everyone out at 6:00 so there will be plenty of time for the actors to take their positions for the opening at 8:30."

"We'll do our best to guard the props," Mandy said.

"Thanks," Aunt Julie replied. "Actually, with more people around, there's less chance of things being tampered with. The volunteers will be told to keep a lookout too."

After they had parked, they headed for the Visitors' Center. Peyton completed a perfect cartwheel and then rushed up to them.

"Hi, guys. Are you going to Fright Night tonight?" When they both nodded, she frowned. "I wish I could go, but Mom says I'm too young. It's not fair."

Julie winked at her. "Just wait a couple of years, Punkin. Your mother doesn't want you to have bad dreams. Some of the actors look pretty gruesome." She entered the Visitors' Center.

Mandy gave the little girl a quick hug. "We'll tell you all about it. Nick's kind of hoping it doesn't give *him* bad dreams, right Nick?"

He scowled at her. "They couldn't look any worse than *you* do first thing in the morning."

She crossed her eyes and stuck out her tongue at him. "Come on. We've got work to do. First, though, we're going to see if we can find that secret tunnel."

Inside the fort, they checked all four corners of the parade grounds.

"I don't see any hole that could be an entrance," Nick said. "Could it be disguised as something else?"

"I don't know," replied Mandy. "Maybe we can find where it comes out down by the water. Come on."

They trooped out through the main entrance and over to the Battery B doghouse. They clattered down the stairs. Nick stuck close to the girls, hoping he wouldn't see the ghost soldier again. He made a point of *not* looking around, just in case the phantom lurked in the shadows.

Down by the river they followed the edge of the waterfront, looking for any kind of entrance into the ground, but no luck.

"It doesn't make sense anyway," Nick said. "Fort builders wouldn't make an escape tunnel come out right where the enemy ships would be. That's like going from the frying pan into the fire. The exit would have to be kind of hidden."

"What about those woods over there?" Peyton asked. Farther along the waterfront, a stand of trees grew between the shore and the outer wall of the fort. As they got closer, she said, "Look, a path! Let's follow it."

The trail wound through the forest, going uphill. It was cool in the shade and very quiet. They walked along in single file, their footsteps muffled by the groundcover of old pine needles.

Mandy came to a sudden stop. "I don't believe it. There it is!"

The children stared at a dark hole off the right side of the path. Granite blocks framed the opening and weeds grew up in front of it.

"Cool!" said Nick. "Does anyone have a light?"

"Of course I do," Mandy replied. She dug out her penlight and handed it to him. "I want it back."

"So why don't *you* look in the hole?" Nick said, "Since the light is yours."

Mandy crossed her arms. "Well, I thought *you* wanted to look."

He grinned at her. "You're afraid there might be snakes in there, aren't you? Didn't you tell me once there are no poisonous snakes in Maine?"

"Yes," she said, "but it doesn't matter. You go ahead and look."

Still grinning, Nick lay on his stomach and stuck his head close to the hole. He turned on the light. "I can't see far—the light's not strong enough—but it's definitely a tunnel!"

"Can you go in any deeper?" Peyton asked.

"Uh, it's not very wide. I might get stuck." Nick shimmied away from the hole and sat up. "Do you want to try? You're a lot smaller."

"Sure!" Peyton clicked on her light.

"Wait!" said Mandy. "What if *you* get stuck? We wouldn't be able to get you out."

"I'll just go a little way. If it gets tight, I'll stop."

Nick and Mandy held their breath as Peyton crawled into the tunnel. They could just see the bottoms of her sneakers. She stayed in one place for a minute or so and then backed out.

"The tunnel goes up," she said. "I could see a little bit of light at the end."

"Could this be how the intruder is getting in?" Nick asked, puzzled. "I really don't think a grownup could fit in there."

"Plus, the tunnel isn't long enough to come out up in the courtyard," Mandy added.

"You wouldn't be able to see sky through it from here."

"Let's see where the path goes," Peyton suggested.

At a trot, they followed the trail out of the woods and up to the wall of the fort. They climbed over and hopped down, and found themselves a short distance from the big cannon.

"We're at Battery A!" said Mandy.

"Hey, look at that," Nick said. He walked over to a hole in the ground. Just like the one in the woods, it was lined with granite. Chunks of stone had been placed in the hole to partially block it. "I didn't notice this when we were here the other day. I bet this is where the tunnel starts. They must have put these rocks in here to keep kids from trying to crawl through."

"Are you sure this is it?" asked Mandy. "I'll go back down to the other hole and yell into it. See if you can hear me."

A few minutes later Nick heard a faint 'hello.' After glancing around to make sure no one except Peyton was looking, he put his mouth close to the hole and shouted back, "I hear you!"

Mandy returned and the three of them stood around the hole. "So what could the tunnel be for?" she asked.

"Well, it *could* have been a secret way to escape if they had made it big enough for men to fit through," said Nick.

"But they didn't," Mandy replied.

Peyton raised her hand like she was in school. "Maybe they rolled cannon balls down the tunnel that would come out the other end and knock down enemies just like bowling pins!"

Nick chuckled. "Not a bad idea, but they would just jump out of the way." He snapped his fingers. "I bet I know! See how the ground is low here where the hole is? It must be a sort of drain. If it rained really hard, they wouldn't have wanted water rising up around the cannons."

The girls thought about it.

"That makes sense," Mandy said, "but it's kind of disappointing. I was hoping for something more exciting."

"Me too," agreed Peyton. "So we still don't know where the *real* secret tunnel is."

"No, but we don't have time to look right now. We better get up to the Officers' Quarters as fast as we can. We don't want anything bad to happen in the fort while we're out here exploring."

Nick trailed behind the girls as they scrambled up the steep hillside to the top of the ramparts and then hurried down the stairs to the postern door. He sure wished he didn't have to go back in there. He had a bad feeling. Would the witch with the 'evil eye' be waiting for him? Or the old soldier's ghost? Or both?

## Chapter 19. The Hex

"Let's stay together today," Nick suggested, "and just cruise around." He *really* didn't want to be alone in the Officers' Quarters, Two-Step Alley or anywhere else in the fort.

"That's a good idea," said Mandy. "There are tons of people here. No one's going to try to wreck stuff in front of an audience."

All through the casemates, storage rooms, and Officers' Quarters volunteers were busy putting the finishing touch to props for the first Summer Fright Night. The children stood on the parade grounds, watching the action going on all around them.

"I wonder if that guy is one of the actors?" Peyton said, pointing at a tall, slender man dressed in black who seemed to be slinking from one casemate to the next. He had scraggly dark hair and a goatee that came to a point. His hands were stuck in his pockets and he walked without looking around. Peyton wrinkled her nose. "He kind of looks like the devil."

"Hey, I've seen him before," said Nick. "He walked through there on Monday. I thought it was strange he didn't stop to look at the cannon."

"He's acting suspicious, don't you think?" Mandy said in a low voice. "Let's follow him."

They climbed up into the nearest casemate and followed the man by keeping close to the pillars. When he got to the last casemate, he disappeared.

"Shoot!" said Mandy. "Which way did he go?"

They stood at the landing between stairs going down to the dry moat outside and stairs going up to the Officers' Quarters, the same spot they had been in before when searching for the elusive figure.

"You go down, we'll go up!" Mandy said.

The girls hurried up the steps to the second floor of the Officers' Quarters.

*Not again*, thought Nick. He plunged down the steps and out the doorway. He caught a glimpse of the back of a black clad leg disappearing into the doorway straight ahead that he now knew led to Long Alley.

"Oh, rats," he muttered. Why couldn't the guy have gone the other way? Nick jogged to the opening and hesitated before stepping inside. Would the man in black be waiting? He took a deep breath and stuck his head inside. A dark figure moved up the lengthy tunnel. Light entering through rifle slots made a pattern of bars on the brick ceiling.

Nick experienced *deja vu*, that feeling of having seen or done something before. Just like yesterday in Two-Step Alley, there was no way he would follow this guy and risk getting attacked. What if it was Drake Duggen? Now that he knew the intruder was also a warlock practicing black magic, it made it even riskier. Nick remembered that Long Alley ran parallel to Two-Step Alley around three sides of the fort. So if the man kept going, he would come out way over by the main gate. The kids could get there before him by running across the parade grounds. He had to find Mandy and Peyton! He dashed back through the arched doorway and up the stone stairs.

The girls stood at the top, waiting for him.

"He didn't go in Two-Step," Mandy said. "Did you see him, Nick?"

"Yes! He's in Long Alley. Come on, let's beat him to the other end!" Nick scrambled down the stairs to the courtyard and raced across the grass, with the girls right behind him.

As they approached the far corner by the tower, Mandy said, "Wait, Nick, slow down. We don't want him to see us!"

The children slowed to a quick walk.

"Where does the tunnel come out?" Nick asked.

"I'll show you," said Peyton, "this way." She led them through several doorways, past the end of Two-Step Alley, and through another arched door to the outside. In the dry moat, they stood in front of the door to Long Alley.

"Someone needs to take a look and see if he's coming," said Nick. *And it won't be me*, he added silently.

"I'll do it!" Peyton volunteered. She stepped inside and then out again. "The tunnel bends to the left. I'll have to go in a little ways." She returned in a few minute. "Nobody yet."

A sudden thought hit Nick. "What are we going to do when he gets here? If this guy is Drake Duggen, he's dangerous!"

"We'll follow him and see what he does," said Mandy. "We just need to make sure he doesn't see *us*."

Nick swallowed hard. "We're in plain sight. Don't you think we should hide?"

"I know a good place!" Peyton said. "Come on." She ducked through the doorway and led them into a dark room right near the bend in the tunnel, one of the many powder magazines.

"This is perfect," Mandy said in a low voice. "We'll be able to see him, but he can't see us."

"We hope," Nick muttered. His heart thumped like a piston. Surely the guy would be able to hear it. He put a hand on his chest and pressed, trying to quiet the wild beating.

Footsteps echoed in the corridor. It was hard to tell how far away the man was. They wouldn't be able to see him until he reached the bend.

"I think he's getting closer," Peyton whispered.

"Shhh," warned Mandy.

A moment later, the man clattered down the stairs and passed the powder magazine where they watched. The children sidled out of the room and peered around the corner. The man stood in front of the outside door, a black silhouette against the light.

"All set for tonight," he murmured. "These ignorants who want to get creeped out will have a night to remember, that's for sure. I'll teach them a lesson about mocking the dark arts." He snickered. "As for those interfering kids, I've got a little surprise for them."

Nick covered his mouth to stifle a gasp. Did the guy know they were right there?

The man began to mutter. He raised his left hand to the wall as if writing something. His voice, vibrating with power and menace, strengthened so they could hear what he was saying.

"I watch with my eye
A dark spirit spy
You cannot escape
Asleep or awake."

He gave an evil cackle and then stepped outside into the dry moat.

Mandy, with Peyton right behind her, slipped over to the doorway. "He drew another eye," she whispered, pointing at the wall. She took a quick look out the door. "He's gone. Come on!"

Nick lagged behind, his stomach churning as he thought about the hex the warlock had just put on them. He would be watching *them* wherever they went. And he had a surprise for them—obviously, not a *good* surprise. Nick gulped. He was doomed. Realizing he was alone, he quickened his pace to catch up with the girls. He found them on the parade grounds.

"We looked around, but it's like the guy vanished," said Mandy.

"Maybe he left," said Peyton.

"From the way he talked, he's got something nasty planned for tonight," Mandy said. "He's going to try to ruin Fright Night. We'd better warn Aunt Julie."

"Worse than that, he's got something planned for *us*," Nick said in a tight voice. He didn't even want to *think* about what it might be.

## Chapter 20. Fright at the Fort

"So this is it," said Mandy. "Fright Night is here at last."

After a quick supper of Chinese take-out, Nick and Mandy were hanging out in the Visitors' Center, watching the volunteer actors in costumes checking in and being assigned a spot in the fort.

A couple of tall aliens walked in together and were directed by Julie to the Officers' Quarters. They were followed by a zombie mother and daughter with oozing sores on their faces and fake blood around their mouths. They were sent to the north entrance of Two-Step Alley.

Nick felt a delicious shiver crawl along his spine at the thought of the many gruesome creatures that would be 'haunting' the fort tonight—a ghoul around every corner. It would be a barrel of fun if they didn't have to worry about the intruder.

"Aunt Julie took a look around this afternoon after we told her about the man in black," Mandy said, "but she didn't find anything except the red eye symbols. She's pretty worried. Friends of the Fort couldn't cancel the event with the amount of advance tickets already sold. She's telling all the volunteers to keep a lookout for troublemakers."

"As if they could tell the difference between a fake witch and a real one," Nick said. "I have a bad feeling about the whole thing."

Mandy put her hands on her hips. "Aunt Julie knows what Drake Duggen looks like. She said Brooke went to high school with him and he was strange even back then. Without mentioning his name, she's giving everyone a description of him. Also, there's a police officer and EMT here."

Nick shook his head. "So all he has to do is wear a disguise and blend in with the spooks. The guy is evil and he's determined to wreck things. With his power, no one can stop him."

"Don't be such a downer, Nick!" Mandy exclaimed. "We won't let anything happen."

"What can *we* do?" argued Nick. "Julie says after our tour, we have to come right back here to stay safe." Secretly, he was *very* glad about that.

Mandy's mouth set in a stubborn line. "I'll think of something."

When all of the actors had received their assignments, Julie turned to Mandy and Nick. "Okay, you two. You will be in the first group. Your guide is Turner." She pointed to a tall, gangly teenager dressed in a butler outfit complete with black bowtie. "I want you to stay close to him at all times. When your tour is over, come right back here and report to me. I have doubts about letting you go, but I know how much you've been looking forward to this. *Please* be careful. . . promise?"

"Sure we will," Mandy said.

"Yup," agreed Nick. He was excited and nervous at the same time. *Anything* could happen.

As the children followed Turner through the main gate, strobe lights bounced off the stone walls in a dizzying whirl, turning the grinning skeleton in the canoe different colors. A group of fifteen people followed the guide, laughing and pointing. One girl screeched when a dangling spider brushed against her face. Just beyond the archway stood the Grim Reaper, a tall figure robed and hooded in black, holding a sickle on a long pole. As the visitors passed him, he stepped toward the same girl, raising his weapon in a threatening manner. She screamed again and clutched her boyfriend's arm.

"Don't worry, Chloe," said her friend. "The spooks won't hurt you. They aren't allowed to touch us. It's in the rules."

Turner led the group to the right, down to where the casemates started. He climbed the stairs to the first level, where three clowns stood revving chain saws. Nick was relieved to see the chains had been removed from the saws. *It's just pretend*, he reminded himself.

In the next casemate, a woman's body, draped in white, lay in a wooden coffin. As everyone peered in for a closer look, the corpse's eyes opened and she smiled at them, revealing glistening vampire teeth. Several people squealed in surprise and jumped back.

Each casemate held a macabre scene different from the last.

"Isn't this great?" Mandy said to Nick.

He nodded and gave her a lopsided grin. *So far, so good.*

At the last casemate, a trio of witches, one of them a man, cackled and chanted around a bubbling black cauldron. The warlock had a short pointed beard. Nick began to sweat. *Was it Drake Duggen?* Smoke rose from the pot in wispy clouds, partially hiding the hideous faces. The man stared at Nick through the mist and his lips moved without sound, as if muttering a curse. *Oh, man*, thought Nick, *he's here!* He took a step back and nudged Mandy, but she shook her head and walked toward their guide, who watched the group with amusement.

"I don't think it's him, Nick," she murmured. "The figure we saw in Long Alley was taller."

"Okay, everyone, this way," said Turner. "We have to keep moving. There's another group coming along right behind us." He led them up the stairs to the second floor of the Officers' Quarters.

More strobe lights flashed. The dummy hanging from the scaffold looked quite real, its head lolling at an awkward angle as if broken. Nick noticed the red eye symbol was still there, which stretched his nerves a little tighter—the all-seeing eye of the witch, watching, waiting.

Their feet clunked on the wooden floor as the group advanced to the next room. This had been set up to look like a laboratory manned by aliens. The pale creatures didn't talk, but their big empty eyes gazed at the visitors in a creepy way. Several humans strapped to gurneys groaned and called out for help. Obviously, they were 'guinea pigs' for the aliens' experiments.

Nick was glad to escape from that room, but he shivered when he realized where they were headed—up the stairs to Two-Step Alley.

"Stay in single file, but close together," Turner directed. "We'll be going down two steps about every ten feet, so be careful. It's very dark in here." The sounds of creaks, groans and growls filled the tunnel.

"It must be a recording," Mandy whispered to Nick. "This is so cool."

Nick thought Two-Step Alley was scary enough without any special effects. They passed a rifle port where a red light glowed on a big, hairy tarantula. On another windowsill, the beady eyes of a rat glittered. It was similar to the one they had found with its head cut off, but this one had stayed in one piece. A red eye symbol gleamed on the rat's side. Nick moaned. *Not again.*

As the group rounded the last bend in the long passageway, gunfire echoed through the chamber, making everyone gasp and duck down.

"It's okay," said the guide in a voice that trembled a little. "Just part of the show. Follow me." He shuffled down the last stretch of Two-Step, his flock close on his heels.

As they burst out of the tunnel, everyone talked at once.

"That sure sounded real!" said the girl Chloe to her boyfriend.

"I don't think I can take much more," the girl said, sniffling. "It's a lot scarier than I thought."

"Oh, come on, Chloe," he replied. "I'll protect you." He put his arm around her and pulled her close. "Okay?"

Straight ahead, a spotlight flared on the mother and daughter zombies who sat on the stone floor with their backs against the wall. The blood on their faces glistened in the light. As the visitors filed past them, the 'living dead' hissed and reached out with claw-like fingers.

"That's it," said Chloe, "I'm done. Let's go, Zach."

Protesting, her boyfriend followed her out toward the main gate. Nick would have happily joined them.

"We're halfway into the tour—hope you're having fun!" said Turner. "This is my first time as a guide. Some of this stuff is a surprise to me too." He led them through a dirt-floored storeroom set up as a corn maze where more ghastly ghouls were hanging out. "Okay, we've saved the best for last," he said, rubbing his hands together. "They say Long Alley is really haunted, so don't be surprised if you see a genuine ghost!"

They passed the hissing zombies again and stepped outside onto the brick walkway beside the dry moat. Fog swirled above the long grassy swath between Two-Step Alley and Long Alley.

"Mother Nature's contribution to Fright Night," Turner said, "*real* fog. You can't beat that!"

They entered the yawning black doorway and turned left. Long Alley seemed dark and quiet, compared to the rest of the fort. Rustlings and whispers made the passageway even spookier than the 'haunted house' soundtrack in Two-Step Alley. Nick gulped. He was standing in the spot where Drake Duggen had put the hex on them earlier in the day. He shuddered. He didn't need to look at the wall to know the eye symbol was still there, the 'dark spirit spy.' The witch had eyes everywhere.

"Okay, everyone, follow me," the guide said. "Watch your step."

Here and there along the tunnel, a dim light showed. The blocks of granite below the rifle slots hunkered like brooding trolls. A few yards along, a chef jumped out at them with an evil laugh, waving a bloody meat cleaver. Several people screamed. Farther down, a headless man in a black suit stood on a stone block. In his hand he held a head by its black hair.

After the passageway with the stone blocks, they entered an even longer section. It seemed to go on forever. Finally, a few steps took them up to a room made for cannons. There crouched a grotesque gargoyle with stubby black wings and a skull face. As Nick and Mandy sidled past it, the creature's eyes glowed bright yellow and it growled at them. An aura of evil seemed to surround it. The eyes hypnotized Nick and his feet felt too heavy to move.

"Come on, Nick," Mandy murmured, grabbing his arm and pulling him along. "I don't like that guy."

The last person in the group had just passed the gargoyle, when a tormented scream ripped the air. A teenage boy behind Nick dropped to the ground and lay writhing on the floor. "Ow, ow," he howled.

"Good grief!" said Mandy. "What happened?"

"I don't know," Nick yelled.

They stepped away from the boy so the guide could get to him. Turner snapped on a flashlight and crouched down beside the twitching boy. "What's wrong?" he asked in a panicky voice. "Is he having an epileptic fit?"

The boy curled into a fetal position and stopped moving.

"Oh, no," Turner whispered. "Is he. . .? We need to get help!"

"That's my brother Ben," said an older teen, kneeling beside him. "Come on, buddy, wake up!"

Before anyone could run for the EMT, the boy sat up. "Caleb? Wh-what happened?" he asked.

"Are you okay, Ben?" Turner asked him.

"I th-think so. I feel kind of dizzy and tingly. It was like getting an electric shock."

"Can you walk?" said his brother. He helped him up. "We'll get you out of here. Can someone hold his other arm?"

Nick stepped forward to help. They supported Ben as they all shuffled along the last stretch of tunnel to the exit. Nick glanced over his shoulder for one last look at the gargoyle, but he was gone. *That's strange*, thought Nick. *Why would an actor leave before the other groups have come through?*

By the time they reached the end of Long Alley, the boy was able to walk on his own. "I still think you should be checked out by a medic," said Turner. "There's one at the Visitors' Center. Mandy and Nick, would you go with them? I've got to meet another group at the main gate."

"Sure," said Mandy.

The rest of the group took the stairs up out of the moat and over the ramparts to the parking lot, chattering with excitement. Mandy and Nick led Ben and Caleb across the courtyard. The fog made everything look even more mysterious. An explosion boomed from the roof of the fort.

"Are they firing the cannon?" Nick asked, puzzled.

"No, they wouldn't do that!" exclaimed Mandy.

Another boom split the air, and then another. Sparks rained down on them from above.

"Yow! Take cover!" yelled Mandy.

The four of them ran for the main gate. A group of people waiting for the next tour stood under the archway. Just as Mandy and Nick got there, a running figure in black with stubby wings bouncing on its shoulders shoved Nick from behind. The guy pushed his way through the crowd.

"It's the gargoyle!" shouted Nick. "Let's go!"

They scrambled after the man, but he was too fast for them.

Outside the gate, the gargoyle vanished in the fog.

## Chapter 21.  Captured!

"That was quite the Fright Night," Aunt Julie said the next morning. "More frightful than planned, but it's over, thank goodness. I just hate to think that Drake Duggen—if it was him—got away with tasering a poor kid. I couldn't believe it when the EMT found prong marks on his arm. I'm glad the boy is okay."

Nick finished chewing a piece of bacon and set down his fork. "I'm glad too. I think the taser was meant for me though. Remember, Mandy, we heard the warlock say he had a surprise for us? I think that was it. I did some research online last night when we got back.

There's a type of taser that can shoot a charge fifteen feet and immobilize a person for 30 seconds. Ben stepped behind me at the wrong moment and took the hit. He looked like he was in agony." Nick swallowed hard.

"I'm sorry he had to go through that," said Mandy. "Hopefully, now that Fright Night is over, Drake Duggen will stay away from the fort."

Julie sighed. "At least until October when we gear up for the *big* Fright at the Fort. I don't even want to think about that right now. With the relatives arriving today and the Ghost Tour at the fort tonight, I've got enough to think about. I'm so glad I have the day off."

"When is everyone getting here?" Nick asked.

"Well, your parents and sister are flying into Bangor this afternoon and my sister Ronda is already in the area with little Noah."

Just then Julie's cell phone rang. Her eyes widened as she listened to the voice on the other end. "I'll be right over!" She grabbed her car keys off the hook. "Come on," she said, "that was the volunteer who opened the fort this morning. They've got a guy dressed in a gargoyle suit locked up in the Battery B powder magazine!"

Nick and Mandy stared at each other. "Gargoyle?" they both said.

"It must be Drake Duggen!" Nick exclaimed.

"How did *that* happen?" Mandy asked.

"We'll soon find out!" said Julie, heading out the door.

That evening the relatives gathered at Aunt Julie's house for supper.

"It's so good to see you!" Mandy exclaimed, giving Nick's sister Christianne a hug. "You too, Noah." They bumped fists. "You won't believe what's been going on."

"It's crazy," said Nick, jumping in. "This guy who's a male witch was getting into the fort and wrecking things set up for Fright Night. Last night he dressed up like a gargoyle with glowing yellow eyes." Nick shuddered at the memory. "He hit a boy in our group with a taser in Long Alley and then he set off explosions on top of the fort."

"That must have been scary," Christianne said. "Did they catch him?"

"Not until this morning," Mandy said. "His boat was still tied up at the fort wharf. He must have run down the Battery B stairs last night but didn't make it out. The volunteer who opened the fort today found a guy in a gargoyle costume locked up in the powder magazine, yelling his head off. With him, he had the taser, a

UV flashlight, and a remote control to set off the explosives."

Nick interrupted her. "It turns out he wore special contact lenses that glowed in the dark when he shined the UV light on them—very spooky. I'd like to try that for Halloween! You can buy the stuff online. Anyway, when we got there, we discovered the door to the dungeon, which is usually open, had been slammed shut and secured with a chain and ancient lock. Julie said she had never seen the lock before. Drake Duggen was babbling that someone pushed him into the room and locked it, but he couldn't see anyone.

"How did you get him out?" Noah asked, his blue eyes wide. "Did you have a key?"

"No," Mandy replied. "The police used a tool to cut the chain. Drake Duggen is in jail now."

"I missed all the excitement last night," Peyton said, "but not tonight! Mom said I can go on the Ghost Tour with you. I'm bringing Sergeant Hegyi's keys. Can you get them down, Nick?"

Nick reached up to the deer antler to snag the ring of keys. "Here you go," he said, handing them to Peyton.

Christianne said, "I'm glad Mom and Dad are letting me do the Ghost Tour too." She tossed her long brown hair over her shoulder. "It's going to be *so* cool." She smiled at Peyton. The two girls had hit it off the moment they met.

"Will we really see a ghost?" Noah asked. "Or will it be fake like Fright Night?"

Nick crossed his arms. "I might have seen one already. In fact, it was right where Drake Duggen got locked up. It was a soldier who looked just like a photo of Sergeant Hegyi, who was caretaker of the fort back in the late 1800s."

Mandy locked eyes with Nick. "Do you think it was Sergeant Hegyi's ghost who captured the witch last night? It would sure make sense. With Drake Duggen setting off explosions, the Sergeant would consider him an enemy of the fort."

Nick gave a nervous laugh. "How could a ghost lock someone up?"

"You'd be surprised what ghosts can do," Noah replied. "I hope I get to see him."

"Better you than me, kid," Nick muttered under his breath. A chill tingled down his back as he recalled that Noah had been an *ultra* ghost magnet in their last adventure in St. Augustine, Florida. He had actually sat at the kitchen table having milk and cookies with a boy ghost named Charles. No telling what would happen with *him* around.

At 7:30 p.m. adults and children piled into several vehicles and headed for Fort Knox. A volunteer had let the East Coast Ghost Trackers in earlier to set up their equipment.

"We have a surprise for you," Aunt Julie said, as they gathered round her in the Visitors' Center. "Because there are so many youngsters in tonight's group, the Ghost Trackers offered to do a private tour just for you from 8:00 to 9:00. Eight is the minimum age for the tours, so we think you can all handle it. The ghost hunters said children have a special energy that often makes contact with spirits easier, so they're eager to try."

Nick closed his eyes for a moment. *Great, just great. The ghosts will be babbling their heads off. Oops, bad expression. I don't want to see a ghost at all, but one with no head would be even worse.*

## Chapter 22. Ghost Tour

"Wake up, Nick," said Mandy, nudging him. "They're here!"

He opened his eyes to see four men and two women troop into the room, dressed like a SWAT team in black vests and camo pants. They arranged themselves in a semi-circle in front of the children. The oldest guy, Ken, introduced the others.

"We're excited to work with you kids tonight," Ken said. "Right after Fright Night, there's always a lot of action among the spirits at the fort. Maybe they absorb energy from the crowds and their emotions. I want to reassure you that all the entities we have communicated with here are friendly, so you have nothing to fear."

"Is one of them Sergeant Leopold Hegyi?" Mandy asked, crossing her fingers.

"There have been a number of sightings of a tall figure in a dark cape who we think is Leopold," Ken replied. "His favorite area seems to be Two-Step Alley. He has the strongest reason of anyone to be attached to the fort, having walked his rounds here twice a day for thirteen years. We keep hoping he will try to get through to us."

With a spark of interest, Nick noticed electronic gadgets on the table. "Are these the things you use to find ghosts?"

Another ghost hunter named Jamie stepped forward. "Yes, and we'll be using them once we enter the fort. This is a K-2 sensor," he said, picking up a device about the size of a television remote control. "Static electricity makes the light change color." He demonstrated by putting his other hand about six inches above the sensor, which caused the light to flicker from green to red. "This is what happens when a spirit is present."

"Another tool we use," Ken said, "is a ghost box." He pointed to a rectangular object with knobs. "It's a modified radio receiver that sweeps through AM or FM radio bands. Spirits can be heard within the static between bands."

"They talk to you?" Noah asked with interest. "I had a ghost friend in Florida who talked to me all the time until he got reunited with his mother and father. I kind of miss him."

"Noah could even see him," Christianne exclaimed, "but I couldn't."

Ken and Jamie exchanged glances and grinned.

"This is going to be interesting," said Jamie. "Let's get started."

The Ghost Trackers led the way to the main gate of the fort and along the edge of the parade grounds to the Officers' Quarters. Most of the stuff from Fright Night had already been removed by volunteers. The group filed through the door of the first floor room that held the exhibit of antique stuff surrounded by the black fence. Beneath a square opening in a brick wall, a row of dolls sat on the floor.

"Oh, dolls!" exclaimed Peyton. "They're so pretty. Which one is your favorite, Christianne?"

As the little girls whispered together, Nick scowled. "What do dolls have to do with ghosts?" he asked Mandy.

"I'm sure we'll find out," she replied.

"We've often made contact with the spirit of a young girl named Elizabeth," explained Jamie. "We think she's around four or five years old. We don't know why she haunts the fort.

Maybe her family lived in a house here before the fort was built. Sometimes we can get her to play games with us." He indicated a shelf above the dolls which held an LED ball and a couple of K-2 sensors. "Hi, Elizabeth," he said, "can you make the ball light up?"

After a few minutes of Jamie talking to the ghost, the sensors on the shelf lit up, turning from green to light orange to orange to red. The ball fell to the floor and rolled a few feet, colors flashing inside of it.

"She wants to play," Jamie said. He placed a K-2 sensor upright in the lap of each doll. "Okay, Elizabeth, I bought you a new doll today, the one with the pretty blue dress. If you like her, can you give her a hug?"

Nothing happened.

"Well, maybe you like one of the other dolls better. Can you show us which one you like?"

"It will be the one with the pink dress!" Peyton whispered.

"I think it's the one with the yellow dress," murmured Christianne.

Nick rolled his eyes. *Why would a ghost care about dolls? It's not as if she can play with one.* His eyes bugged out as three of the sensors started flickering like Christmas lights.

"She likes all of them *except* the new doll," Jamie said, puzzled. "Well, thanks,

Elizabeth. I'll be back later to play more games with you." He gathered up the sensors and handed one to each of the kids. "We're going to move on to Two-Step Alley to see what other spirits we can contact."

As the children started to follow Jamie outside, with his partner Ken bringing up the rear, Noah stopped short. He seemed to listen for a moment.

"Yes, okay," the boy said, "you want me to give Jamie a message?"

Jamie stuck his head back through the doorway to see what was causing the holdup. He noticed the startled look on Ken's face. "What's up?"

Ken shook his head. "Noah, you tell him."

"Elizabeth held onto my arm, like she didn't want me to go. She told me to tell you, Jamie, that she likes the new doll. She just wanted to tease you. She says thank you for giving her dolls and for playing with her. She's pretty lonely."

Jamie stared at Noah in amazement. "She told you all that? Can you see her?"

"Sure," Noah replied, "she's right over there. She's kind of shy." He pointed to the far corner of the room.

"This is awesome," murmured Ken. He locked eyes with Jamie for a moment. "What does she look like?" he asked Noah.

Noah waved at the ghost that only he could see. "She's smaller than me with wavy brown hair, a blue hair ribbon and a long blue dress with a ruffle on the bottom."

"Incredible," Jamie muttered. He waved at the invisible girl. "Hi, Elizabeth. I'm glad you like the dolls." He turned back to Noah. "Noah, I hope we can keep you around for awhile. You're a pipeline for the spirits to communicate with us. This is amazing! I can't wait to see what happens in Two-Step Alley."

Nick shook his head. A feeling of dread weighed down his stomach like a lead cannonball. What *would* happen in Two-Step Alley? He was afraid to find out.

## Chapter 23. The Ghost Speaks

Ken led the group outside and then back through another doorway in the Officers' Quarters. A flight of stairs took them up to the entrance of Two-Step Alley.

Nick shivered. This might be Sergeant Hegyi's favorite place, but it sure wasn't Nick's. Thank goodness he was in the middle of the pack with Ken, Mandy and Noah ahead and Christianne, Peyton and Jamie behind. He should be safe. And thank goodness Drake Duggen was behind bars.

"Be as quiet as you can," Ken warned in a low voice. "Lights off and hold your sensor out in front of you. Once we get around the corner, we'll stop and let our eyes get used to the dark." After they had all made the bend, the Ghost Trackers snapped off their lights.

In a few minutes, Nick could see the long corridor stretching out in front of them. A bit of light from outside filtered through the rifle ports, creating a mysterious passageway of grayness and inky shadows. Way down at the next corner, a red light cast a dim glow. Was it left over from Fright Night?

"What's making that red light?" Peyton whispered to Jamie.

"The Trackers set it up," the man explained in a low voice, "so we can see if anything passes in front of it."

The distant light had a hypnotic effect, drawing Nick's eyes like a magnet. He almost dropped his K-2 sensor when the device started flickering from green to red. The sensors held by the others also flashed.

"Don't move," Jamie said. "There's a spirit here."

Nick gulped. He couldn't move if he wanted to. Staring again at the faraway gleam, he noticed a black hole in the middle of it. It seemed to waver and change shape.

"It's coming this way," Ken whispered.

As it got closer, they could make out the outline of a man. Though he appeared to be walking, no sound of footsteps echoed in the tunnel. He stopped about twenty feet away. This was no guy in a costume.

"Hello, who's there?" Ken said out loud. "Is it you, Mike? Can you touch one of us?"

Nothing happened.

"Mike is one of our regular spirit contacts here at the fort," Jamie explained in a low voice. "He's somewhat of a prankster. He likes to pull hair and pinch people."

The figure in front of them just stood there, as if listening.

"I'll turn on the ghost box," said Ken. "Can you tell us who you are?" He turned a dial that squawked through various frequencies. A line of a pop song blared from the radio, sounding out of place. From a sea of static, a few words came through in a robotic voice.

"Did you hear that?" Jamie asked the group. "Was that *lee po*?"

"Leopold," said Ken. "It's Ordnance Sergeant Hegyi!"

Cold sweat dribbled down Nick's back. He was seeing and hearing a real ghost!

"Key," said the voice.

Peyton squeaked, "Does he want his keys?" She hid them behind her back.

More words followed. "Box. . . letter."

Ken spoke up. "Leopold, there's a letter in a box? Is that right?"

"Letter. . . yes. . . read."

Another word came from the ghost box. "Stone."

"Stone?" Ken asked. "What stone do you mean? Can you tell us more?"

"Grave," said the voice.

"Grave?" Ken repeated. "Stone? Someone's gravestone?"

Faintly, they heard one more word that sounded like "Help."

The spirit glided toward them, a looming dark shadow. Everyone gasped. Then it seemed to pass through their group and vanish.

A cold breeze chilled the back of Nick's neck. He squeezed his eyes shut and hugged himself, trying not to pass out.

"Wow," Jamie said under his breath. "That's the best spirit encounter we've ever had. So there's something about a letter and a gravestone. I wonder what he wants help with. Noah, did Sergeant Hegyi tell you anything?"

"No words this time," the little boy replied, "just feelings and pictures. He seemed to be really sad and very, very tired."

"He's been walking these corridors a long time," Ken said. "It's no wonder he's tired. Can you describe the pictures you saw?"

"At first it was somewhere here in the fort. There was a wood floor and a fireplace, like the room we were in with Elizabeth."

"The Officers' Quarters!" Mandy said.

Noah continued. "Then I saw a cemetery with old gravestones. Down at the back next to some trees there was a white stone all by itself. Beside it, a small American flag was stuck into the ground."

"Could you see the name on it?" Mandy asked.

"It was his, Sergeant Hegyi's, with no date, just U.S.A. under his name."

"Hmmm," murmured Ken. "I wonder why he showed you his grave." He turned on his flashlight. "Isn't the old sergeant buried in a cemetery a few miles up the road, Jamie?"

"Yes, that's what we heard." Jamie scratched his head. "If I remember correctly, when he died, his wife in New York didn't want his remains. Someone local donated a plot for him to be buried in."

"I wonder why he's so sad," Peyton said. "We *have* to help him."

Nick still stood like an ice sculpture. Even his insides felt frozen. A ghost had blown through him. He would never be the same again.

"Can we go check the fireplace?" Mandy asked.

Ken shined the light on his watch. "No time. We have a group of thirty adults to take on the next Ghost Tour. They're waiting at the Visitors' Center."

"You go ahead," Jamie said. "I'll take the kids to the Officers' Quarters for a quick look. I'll have them out of there before you arrive with the tour."

"Okay," replied Ken. "Good luck."

Jamie and the children hurried up Two-Step Alley and down the stairs to the Officers' Quarters. "There are fireplaces upstairs and down," he said. "Any idea which one it is?"

Noah squinted in thought. "There's one on the first floor behind that black metal fence, right? In the room where we were playing with Elizabeth? I don't think that's it."

"That leaves seven others," said Jamie. "Let's try up here."

They walked to the nearest fireplace and stood in front of it.

"Why is it green inside the fireplace?" Christianne asked.

"That's algae," explained Jamie. "This hasn't been used for a long time and it feels damp." He ran his hand over the bricks. "Nothing seems loose. Of course, it's probably been re-mortared since Sergeant Hegyi's day to keep it from falling apart."

"So any loose bricks might have been cemented over?" Nick asked, disappointed. He could finally breathe again. Encountering a real ghost had knocked the air right out of him, but now he was as curious as everyone else about Sergeant Hegyi's message.

The opening of the fireplace was about 30 inches high. Peyton ducked her head and stepped into it. She reached up inside and felt around. "Hey, there's kind of a shelf here. There's a lot of crumbly cement on it." She snapped on her light and peered in. "This would sure make a good hiding place."

"If no one lit a fire," Nick said in a dry voice. "No guarantee of that."

"Do you hear the voices outside?" Jamie asked. "The other group has arrived. Come on. You'll have to continue the search tomorrow."

He led them down the stairs to the casemates. They met the large group of adults in the corner of the parade grounds.

"Hi, Mom, hi, Dad!" Christianne called to her parents.

"Hi, Ronda!" Noah said, with a wave.

"Uh, Ronda," Ken said, "is there any chance we could have Noah tag along with the adult group, since you're here? He seems to have a special gift for communicating with the spirits."

"Oh, really?" said Ronda. "Actually, I'm not surprised. When he stayed with me at my inn in Florida, I kept thinking he was talking to an invisible friend. That explains a lot. I always suspected the Crow's Nest Inn was haunted." She grinned at Noah. "Ghosts are good for business."

"Not fair," grumbled Christianne to her mother. "Why can't we all stay?"

"Stop complaining and go with the others," Ariel said. "You had your turn."

Jamie escorted the children, minus Noah, to the door of the Visitors' Center. "Would you kids like to go to the cemetery tomorrow afternoon if we get your parents' permission? We could take a look at that gravestone."

"Sure," said Mandy. "I'd like to see where Sergeant Hegyi is buried."

"Maybe we can find out why he's so sad," Peyton said.

Nick hoped the ghost didn't haunt the cemetery too.

## Chapter 24. The Key to the Mystery

In the morning, the five children headed to the fort with Aunt Julie and Brooke.

"It's such a relief we don't have to worry about intruders and Fright Night anymore," said Julie. "It turns out Drake Duggen was getting into the fort with a key. His girlfriend's mother is a volunteer and she hangs her keys by her kitchen door so she won't forget them. Drake 'borrowed' them for a few hours to have them copied."

"Good grief, he had his own key?" Mandy said. "No wonder it was easy for him. So he didn't use the secret tunnel after all."

Brooke laughed. "There's no secret tunnel. In the old days a sewer line ran from the corner of the parade grounds to the river and sometimes boys would crawl in there and get stuck. The ranger would have to pull them out. It was bricked up a long time ago. It's just inside the doorway to the right of the Officers' Quarters."

"*That's* why we couldn't find it," Nick exclaimed. "I can't wait to see it!"

As they pulled into the parking lot, Julie said, "So, kids, just enjoy yourselves this morning. Show Christianne and Noah around the fort. Jamie will be coming by after lunch to take you to the cemetery. Brooke will be going with you."

"Will we get to ride in the Ghost Trackers' van?" Noah asked.

"I don't know," Julie replied. "You'll have to wait and see."

The children walked past the Visitors' Center toward the main gate. As they neared the Battery B doghouse, Christianne asked, "Could you show us where the bad guy got locked up?"

"Sure," said Peyton. "It's right down at the bottom of these stairs. Turn on your lights."

Everyone in the group now had their own mini light. The beams bounced off the walls as the kids clattered down the steps. At the bottom, paths branched off in different directions.

"So if you go straight, it takes you right out to where the cannon is," Peyton said. "If you go right, there are more stairs that go down near the wharf."

A shiver rippled across Nick's bare arms as he remembered this was where he had seen the Civil War soldier, probably Sergeant Hegyi's ghost.

"The room where Drake Duggen got trapped is this way."

She turned left and led them over to a dark room with a dirt floor. A heavy black door with an arched top was chained open. Their flashlights revealed a narrow window on the back wall with black metal bars.

"People call these rooms dungeons, but they are actually powder magazines where gunpowder and ammunition were stored if the cannons were being used," Peyton explained.

"Well," said Nick, "it sure makes a good jail. I'm *so* glad Drake Duggen got caught!" His foot hit against something. "Hey, look at this. It must be the old lock Julie mentioned." He held it on the palm of his hand so the others could see it.

"It does look ancient," Mandy said, touching it with a finger. The metal of the lock had turned a light green and was covered with scratches.

"It must be made of bronze or brass," Nick said. "They both have copper in them so they turn green after they've been around awhile, like the Statue of Liberty." He swiveled the rectangle tab on the front, revealing a keyhole shaped like the number 9. The shank on the top was shut. "Too bad we don't have a key."

"But we do," said Peyton, pulling the ring of keys from her jacket pocket. "We're looking for a treasure box today, remember? Hold it still, Nick, and I'll see if any of them work." She chose one of the smaller keys and slid it into the keyhole. "It fits!" She turned the key and the shank opened with a click.

The children stared at each other, open-mouthed.

"Where did you find these keys?" Christianne asked.

"In the hotshot furnace at Battery A," said Mandy. "They're Sergeant Hegyi's for sure! The lock must have been on this door back in the 1800s when he was guarding the fort."

Noah said, "That means if we can find his box, one of these keys will probably open it!"

"Let's go search the other fireplaces!" Peyton said.

They hurried up the stairs, through the main gate and across the parade grounds. Back at the Officers' Quarters, they decided to check the upstairs first. After feeling around the ledge in all four fireplaces, they had found nothing except rubble. They headed down the stairs to the first floor. At the back of the room, Noah stopped in his tracks.

"Wait," he said. "This looks familiar." He stood in front of a small fenced-off area with a drain in the floor. Behind it a window showed a glimpse of the dry moat outside. "What is this?"

"Umm, Mom told me this is a latrine," said Peyton, her cheeks turning pink. "It's like—you know—a toilet."

Nick snorted. "They didn't have much privacy."

"I saw this in the pictures the Sergeant showed me last night," said Noah, thinking hard. "The fireplace was just to let us know what part of the fort to go to. It's close, I can feel it." He took a few steps to the right. An archway opened into a small room. "What's this room for?"

Mandy shrugged. "I've never noticed it before. It's probably just a space for the officers to store stuff."

They crowded in, shining their lights around. The stone walls had ripples of white on them, like flowing water that froze in place.

"Gram said that white stuff is called calcium carbonate," said Peyton. "You can see it all through the fort. Before Friends of Fort Knox fixed the roof, there was water leaking in. It made the calcium in the mortar dissolve and drip, just like in a cave."

"Look, there's a space up here," Nick said, pointing his light into a rough triangular hole about five feet above the floor. He stood on tiptoe to peer in. "It goes back pretty far, a perfect place to hide something small." A cool breeze wafted from the hole onto his face. "I don't see anything though."

"Here's another hole," said Noah, crouching beside the bottom of the opposite wall. "I think this is it. I remember seeing what looked like an ice cave, but it didn't make sense to me last night."

He moved back a little so the others could study the opening. Calcium carbonate had flowed around it and it really did look like a miniature ice cave or the door to an igloo. They all lay on the floor, shining their lights inside.

"Cool! Look at the little icicles!" Christianne said.

The white stuff had dripped down the sides of the bricks lining the opening and, in one spot on the overhead bricks, a mini stalactite had formed.

Nick shined his light farther back in the hole. "There's something there. It looks square."

"Can you reach it, Nick?" Peyton asked. "You have the longest arms."

Nick reached into the hole. It was cool in there and again, a light breeze blew across his hand. Probably a ventilation passage, he thought. He grasped the box and pulled it out.

The other children moved in close, shining their lights on the metal box. About the size of a small fishing tackle box, it was spotted with rust and white. The lock holding it shut was similar to the one the kids had discovered in Drake Duggen's dungeon.

"Wow," Mandy said in awe. "We found Sergeant Hegyi's box!"

## Chapter 25. A Grave Injustice

Peyton pulled out the ring of keys. "One of these *has* to fit!" She tried several of the smaller ones before she found the right one. It slid into the keyhole. "Here goes!" She turned it and the lock clicked.

Nick removed the lock and lifted the lid. A thin packet wrapped in oilskin lay inside. He lifted it out and handed it to Mandy. Underneath was a gray cloth bag. "I wonder what this is?" Nick said. "Sergeant Hegyi only mentioned a letter."

"Well, let's read the letter first," said Mandy. She opened the oilskin, revealing a folded piece of paper. The waterproof wrapping had preserved it well. "Shine your lights here." She carefully unfolded the paper and read it out loud.

*To Whom It May Concern*

*Having been in poor health for several years, I wish to make provisions for my death. In the event it should occur while I am still serving at Fort Knox, I elect to be interred locally, so that my wife Louise will not have the expense or trouble of transporting my remains to New York. Ours is an arranged marriage in the sense that she will be able to claim my effects and pension when I pass, in exchange for the years she devoted to caring for my aging parents in Brooklyn while I was away pursuing my Army career. I am grateful to her for that. However, so there will be funds set aside for burial expenses, I have placed what I estimate to be an adequate amount in the box with this letter. When I am failing and know the end is near, I will notify the appropriate person of the box's location. I extend my thanks ahead of time to that person for attending to this matter so that I might rest in peace.*

*Ord. Sgt. Leopold Hegyi*
*January 1, 1900*

"I wonder what happened," said Christianne. "Nobody ever found the letter. . . until now."

"I think I know," said Nick. "Last night after the Ghost Tour I couldn't sleep, so I was looking through that old book in Julie's livingroom called *Fort Knox, Fortress in Maine.* There's a whole chapter about Sergeant Hegyi. He didn't have time to tell anyone about the box. A fisherman noticed the flag hadn't been raised over the fort and when he went to investigate, he found the Sergeant unconscious. He died a little while later from some kind of stroke." Nick lifted the bag out of the box. "It's pretty heavy. Shine your light in here, Noah." He opened the bag. Coins glinted in the light. Nick took one out. "It's a Morgan silver dollar—like the ones we found in the ghost town in Nevada, Mandy!"

"How many are there?" she asked.

"Here, pour them out on my jacket," said Noah, laying his hoodie on the floor.

Nick dumped the coins on the jacket and the children made stacks of five. "Looks like $30," Nick said.

"Is that all?" Christianne asked, disappointed. "That's not much for a treasure."

"Well, they're probably worth about $30 a piece now," said Mandy. "That's, um. . . $900!"

Christianne's face brightened. "Yay, we're rich!" Then she frowned. "Will they let us keep it?"

"Even though we found it, it's not ours," said Noah. "I suppose the money will go to the fort. . . Did you learn anything else about Sergeant Hegyi, Nick?"

"Lots more," Nick replied. "He was born in Hungary and moved to the U.S.A. when he was a teenager. He enlisted in the army and had a pretty interesting life before he came to Fort Knox. He liked horses and trained soldiers in Missouri for the U.S. Cavalry. In fact, some of those soldiers fought with General Custer at the Battle of Bull Run."

"After such an exciting life, it must have been boring for him here," Peyton said. "All he did was walk around an empty fort for thirteen years."

"Yeah," Nick agreed. "His wife came on the train twice a year from Brooklyn, New York to visit him. She brought her two little dogs but didn't even stay with him. She stayed with a family that lived nearby."

"He must have been lonely," said Christianne. "I hope he had a pet too."

Nick nodded. "Actually, the book said he had dogs and about 70 chickens. He used to sell the eggs in Bucksport. He kept a horse in a stable over there and visited it every day. When the river froze in the winter, he would tie a sawhorse to the horse and have it pull him around on the ice."

"That's fun!" Peyton said. "I bet people liked to watch him and his horse. Maybe he wasn't lonely, after all."

"I hope not," Mandy said. She folded the letter and stood up. "We better go give these to Aunt Julie."

The kids put the coins back in the bag and Nick placed it in the box. "Is this what Sgt. Hegyi wanted help with, Noah?" Nick asked.

"I'm not sure," Noah replied, squinting in thought. "I think there's something else."

"Well, maybe we'll figure it out at the cemetery," said Mandy.


After explaining to Julie and Brooke how they had found Sergeant Hegyi's 'treasure,' the children ate lunch, and then piled into the East Coast Ghost Trackers' cool black van.

"So you kids found Leopold's box!" Jamie exclaimed. "That's amazing that he led you right to it."

"We couldn't have done it without Noah," Peyton said, smiling at her new friend.

Brooke said, "I think you're *all* pretty amazing. I didn't really believe in the ghost before, but you've changed my mind."

They rode in the Ghost Trackers' van beneath dark clouds that threatened rain. About a mile and a half up the road, Jamie slowed, did a U-turn and pulled up in front of a graveyard. A wooden sign on a post announced: THE NARROWS CEMETERY. Everyone got out and stood looking around. The old stones leaned in different directions in a rather small cemetery that sloped downhill toward the woods. A few raindrops splattered.

Noah looked up at the sky. "We better hurry. Remember, Sergeant Hegyi's grave is in the back."

"You lead the way, Noah," Jamie said.

They formed a single file behind Noah and walked down toward the trees. He seemed to home right in on a white stone off by itself. Close to it was the small American flag that veterans place on graves of U.S. soldiers. The group stood in a semi-circle in front of the grave. The stone was about 30 inches tall. Inside a shield shape were the raised letters ORD. SGT. LEOPOLD HEYGI, and below the name, U.S.A.

"Why aren't there any dates on the stone?" Peyton asked. "You know, for when he was born and died?"

"I don't know," said Brooke. "There should be. They at least knew the year he died."

"Oh, no," said Nick. "This is even worse. Look at his last name—they mixed up the G and the Y! It's supposed to be H-E-G-Y-I."

"Good grief!" said Mandy, "they spelled his name wrong? No wonder he can't rest in peace!"

"That's why he's so sad," Noah said. "He spent most of his life serving his adopted country and this is what he got."

"This must be what he wants us to help him with!" said Christianne. "Can we fix it?"

"The gravestone belongs to the government and its over a hundred years old, so I doubt if it can be changed," Jamie said.

They all stared at the stone in dismay.

"I have an idea," Peyton finally said. "Maybe we can use the coins the Sergeant left behind to get him a new gravestone. After all, it's his money. Is $900 enough?"

"I think it would be," Brooke replied, "if it wasn't anything fancy. We'll have to check with town officials to see if a new stone is allowed."

"If you look around, you can see some flat granite stones that are pretty simple," said Nick, pointing at one. "We can have his name and dates put on it and lay it in front of the old stone. Then everyone can see how his name is *supposed* to be spelled."

"I think it's a great idea, kids," Jamie said. "I bet one tired old soldier would be eternally grateful."

"We'll take care of it, Sergeant Hegyi," Mandy said in a firm voice. "You can count on us."

Just then, the sun shone through a break in the clouds. A beam focused on the grave like a spotlight.

"He's happy now," said Noah. "The sergeant can finally rest in peace."

*Me too*, thought Nick. *At last, I can enjoy the fort with no evil intruder and one less ghost!*

Ordnance Sergeant Leopold Hegyi
photo: Eva Abbott

**Author's Note: Fact or Fiction?**

Fort Knox is a real place in Maine and all the information about it in the book is true. As a child, I visited it many times with my family and loved exploring the dark tunnels and mysterious rooms. I didn't know much about the history of this impressive fort or the ghosts that supposedly haunt it until I started researching for the story. In the past year I have visited the fort six times, read three books about it, talked with volunteers who work there, and gone on a Ghost Tour through the fort with the East Coast Ghost Trackers.

The few known facts about Ordnance Sergeant Leopold Hegyi made me start wondering about him. What was it like for him to be alone at the fort for 13 years? Why didn't his wife live with him? Why would his ghost haunt the fort? I tried to think of logical answers to those questions. The letter from the Sergeant and coins in the box the children found are made up from my imagination. There *have* been strange sightings in the fort that some people think could be his ghost, but I have seen no ghosts. I visited Sgt. Hegyi's grave and it's true that his last name is spelled wrong and there are no dates on the stone. It seems a poor way to treat a loyal soldier of the U.S. Army and dedicated keeper of the fort.

Fort Knox, along with the amazing Penobscot Narrows Bridge Observatory, is a state park and is owned by the Maine government. The Friends of Fort Knox, an organization of volunteers formed in 1991, have taken over the day-to-day running of the fort and continually put a great deal of effort into raising money for its repair and upkeep. The Fright at the Fort event is their biggest fund-raiser. At this time, however, it is held only in October, not in the summer.

Across the Penobscot River in Bucksport is the cemetery containing the gravestone of Colonel Jonathan Buck where you can see the outline resembling a leg. Next to it is a big white house that was owned by my great-aunt when I was a kid. I was told she was called a witch just because she lived beside the cemetery. I was always fascinated by the stone and would go to look at it whenever my family paid a visit.

I hope you have enjoyed reading *The Fortkeeper's Keys* and will visit Fort Knox soon. . .and don't forget your flashlight!

*~ Angeli Perrow*

Update:  November 2, 2017
On this date a real ceremony with military honors was held at Sgt. Hegyi's grave to dedicate a new granite marker with his birth and death dates and correctly spelled name. A 'grave injustice' made right at last!

# GLOSSARY of Fort Terms

**Barracks:** A building to house soldiers

**Bastion:** A projecting part of a fort for the purpose of shooting cross-fire at the enemy

**Battery:** Guns or cannons placed in a group

**Carriage:** A wheeled frame for carrying a cannon

**Casemate:** A fortified chamber from which guns are fired through openings

**Cistern:** A walled in area for storing drinking water

**Dry Moat:** A ditch around a fort that contains no water

**Fort Keeper:** A soldier, usually a sergeant, in charge of a vacant fort

**Gallery:** A tunnel or underground passage

**Hot Shot:** Solid cannonballs that have been heated before being fired

**Magazine:** A storage area to house guns and ammunition

**Ordnance:** Military weapons, cannons or explosives

**Parade Grounds:** A flat area where military drills are held

**Postern:** A back gate or door in a fort

**Powder Magazine:** A room for storing gunpowder

**Quarters:** Lodgings for military personnel

**Rampart:** The embankment surrounding a fort

**Rodman:** T.S. Rodman, U.S. Army, inventor of the Rodman process of making cannons

# BOOKS BY ANGELI PERROW

## The Key Mystery Series for 8-12 year olds:

*The Lightkeeper's Key*
*The Whispering Key*
*The Ghost Miner's Key*
*The Buccaneer's Key*
*The Outlaw's Key*
*The Fortkeeper's Keys*

## The Celtic Touch Trilogy for teens:

*Celtic Thunder*
*Celtic Tide*
*Celtic Legend*

## Picture Books:

*Captain's Castaway*
*Lighthouse Dog to the Rescue*
*Sirius the Dog Star*
*Many Hands: A Penobscot Indian Story*
  (Lupine Award winner)
*Dogsled Dreamer*
*Love From the Sky*

Learn more at: **www.angeliperrow.com**

## BOOKS ABOUT FORT KNOX

**Fort Knox: Fortress in Maine** by John E. Cayford, CAY-BEL Publishing, 1983.

**The History of America's First FORT KNOX** by Liza Gardner Walsh, Friends of Fort Knox, 2014.

**Haunted Fort: The Spooky Side of Maine's Fort Knox** by Liza Gardner Walsh, Down East Books, 2013.

## OTHER SOURCES OF INFORMATION

**www.friendsoffortknox.org**

**Bucksport Historical Society**
**92 Main St.**
**Bucksport, Maine 04416**
**Open July-August Wed.-Fri. 1-4 p.m.**

**www.eastcoastghosttrackers.com**

**www.youtube.com**
ECGT- Maine's Most Haunted Episode 3: Fort Knox

Made in the USA
Columbia, SC
19 July 2021

42040395R00107